Wicked, wick
through his m

Bill stared at Ellie
drop-dead sexy th
was over her red bikini. Very teasing. Very
exciting. She was all grown-up and hot and
sexy in that get-up. Enough to make a man
howl at the moon.

"   about?" she asked.

With another woman, that question would
have stopped him cold. But with Ellie...
well, it was different. He was tempted to
detail his lusty thoughts to see if she was as
keen to get busy as he was.

"Something about you, Ellie," he said
instead.

The heat from the sun poured down on
them. But it had nothing on the sizzle
between them. Her expression encouraged
him, told him to go for it, to seduce her
into indulging in the kind of no-regrets
wickedness dominating his mind.

With that kind of invitation, who was he to
refuse?

Dear Reader,

I had a challenge with this book – to develop a glam-goth character who's made over into a Malibu beach babe. The latter I understood, having grown up in sunny Southern California and spent time frolicking on its beaches. It was a summer ritual during high school for a bunch of us to rent beach houses (with a few brave-hearted teachers as chaperones) and "hang" in bikinis for a week of flirting, swimming and catching some –

But glam-goth? I was clue— YouTube watching Marilyn Manson and Siouxsie Sioux videos, watched an entire series on Lou Reed, read up on glam-goth makeup and clothes, but it all felt too remote, too distant. Then I found GiGi-D L'Amour, a glam-goth diva extraordinaire, artist and disc jockey who took me under her gothic wing and patiently answered my many questions. Thank you, GiGi!

Also, big thank-yous to two of my favourite authors and good friends, Dawn Atkins and Cindi Myers. Dawn and Cindi are not only talented, but fun to work with! A big thank-you to my editor, Wanda Ottewell, whose guidance and good humour always keep me on track, and to Shaun Kaufman, who diligently read all six story drafts – including the wrong one I gave him accidentally.

So get ready to read about a glam-goth chick in a beach-babe world as she not only experiences a few shock waves, but starts a few of her own…

Happy reading!

Colleen Collins

PS Check out my upcoming books at www.colleencollins.net.

SHOCK WAVES

BY
COLLEEN COLLINS

🌹™ MILLS & BOON®
Pure reading pleasure™

*First published in Great Britain 2008
by Harlequin Mills & Boon Limited,
Eton House, 18-24 Paradise Road, Richmond, Surrey TW9 1SR*

© Colleen Collins 2007

ISBN: 978 0 263 86213 3

14-0708

*Harlequin Mills & Boon policy is to use papers that are
natural, renewable and recyclable products and made from
wood grown in sustainable forests. The logging and
manufacturing processes conform to the legal environmental
regulations of the country of origin.*

*Printed and bound in Spain
by Litografia Rosés S.A., Barcelona*

COLLEEN COLLINS

Deep into the writing, while Colleen Collins was weaving threads of glam-rock and glam-goth into the story, she heard in an old Lou Reed song the name of someone she once knew – Jackie in "Walk on the Wild Side." Jackie Curtis had been her neighbour back in Hollywood, and they used to talk about life and writing and what they wanted to be someday. He was so low-key and easygoing and funny, she had no idea he'd been one of Andy Warhol's superstars until someone told her. And she didn't know he was in "Walk on the Wild Side" until she wrote this book. A tip of the hat to you, Jackie, all these years later.

To GiGi-D L'Amour, who graciously shared her glam-goth world so I could better develop *Shock Waves*' heroine, Ellie. Any inaccuracies are the author's, not GiGi's.

1

COME JOIN the hot, hot, hot Sin on the Beach festival! That's right, beach babes and beach dudes, we're talking hot games, hot competitions, hot bodies to help us kick off the second-season launch of the hottest TV show this season!

Twenty-nine-year-old Ellie Rockwell—glam goth girl, coffee shop owner and serious Lou Reed fan— read the announcement on the kiosk again, certain she was suffering from heatstroke. Or having a heart attack. Or both. Hardly what a woman on her first vacation in five years should be having.

"*Sin on the Beach,*" she murmured, glancing over at the people setting up booths and tents along this stretch of Malibu Beach. It was one thing to read about this festival at her coffee shop, Dark Gothic Roast, located twenty miles inland in fast-paced, hyperstressed Los Angeles, quite another to be standing on the very sand where the TV show was *filmed*.

Everybody and anybody knew better than to call Ellie on Thursday nights between 9:00 and 10:00 p.m. when *Sin on the Beach* aired. She got teased a lot for loving this show, as though goths were narrow-minded enough not to like anything that wasn't black and morbid and reeking of Edgar Allan Poe. Okay, she could do without all the sunshine and tanned bodies on the show, but she dug the buffed actors in Speedos. Especially when they starred in the occasional mystery story line full of shadows and danger. Plus, the night scenes were to die for—moonlight gilding the water, the ocean spilling its secrets and the occasional body onto the shore, the rhythmic tumble of distant, dark waves.

She continued reading. The festival promised games such as Truth or Bare and Hot Shot Photo Scavenger Hunt, surfing competitions, limbo contests, something called Good Vibrations. Even nearby bars were getting into the festival mood by holding karaoke sin-alongs, and...

Her heart stilled.

What was this?

She leaned forward, clutching her black silk top while reading the fine print at the bottom of the poster.

Hey, you! Want to be an extra on Sin on the Beach *and earn beaucoup festival points doing so? Then come to the open audition the first morning of the festival! If you're 18-30, act wicked, dress cool and have a rockin' bod, meet here on Tuesday, August 15, 7:00 a.m. sharp. Be hot, be sinful, be ready!*

For a wild, giddy moment, Ellie imagined herself as an extra on *Sin on the Beach,* looking killer in a black bikini, cavorting in the waves, maybe being the one who found the dead body in a mystery plot and getting to rip loose a bloodcurdling scream. How groovy would that be?

She scanned the ad again. *Wicked, dress cool and have a rockin' bod…*

Her short black hair was wickedly spiked, but she seriously doubted that's the kind of wicked they had in mind. Dress cool? Unless they were into the Mistress of the Dark look, she doubted they'd use that word for her wardrobe, most of it custom-designed by yours truly. Although, lifting everything from cappuccino machines to bags of coffee beans kept her in shape, so humility aside, she could probably pull off the rockin' body.

Wicked. Cool. Rockin'.

She blew out a sigh.

One out of three wouldn't cut it.

Just as well. She expected to hear any day that her business loan had been approved, which meant starting next week she'd begin the expansion of Dark Gothic Roast into the remodeled former warehouse in East L.A. The space was so large, she'd decided to try selling her clothes designs in one of the commercial spaces while overseeing the rental of the others. The enormity of her plans excited and scared the crap out of her. Rather than fret and worry until she got the news, she'd opted to adopt the pragmatic "what happens, happens" attitude.

Until then, she'd chill, do her caretaking thing.

Which meant she needed to ensure her brother, Matt, crossed paths as often as possible with her friend Candy and encourage her other friend Sara to occasionally pry herself off her laptop.

Speaking of which, time to call the mother ship and see how things were going. She flipped open her cell phone and punched in the speed-dial for Sara.

"Hello?"

"It's El. Expecting it was your uncle calling again, hmm? Everything going okay?" She nudged her sunglasses up the bridge of her nose. "Hey, guess who's looking for hot-bodied extras?"

"Johnny Depp?"

"I wish. Seriously, *Sin on the Beach*."

"Cool!"

"Yeah, remember that festival we read about? Well, *Sin* is holding an open audition for extras. Better yet, everybody who gets hired also wins a scad of festival points."

"Ellie Rockwell, I see your name in lights."

"I'm not wicked and cool enough," she muttered.

"What?"

"Nothing. Hey, I'll bring one of these flyers back to the house. There are all kind of games and competitions." And she knew just the people to sign up, too—Matt and Candy.

"Gotta go," Sara suddenly said. "Someone's waiting."

"Tell your Uncle Spence it's your first day on vacation! Girlfriend, you *deserve* a day off."

"Yeah, like you ever close Dark Gothic Roast. Anyway, it's not Uncle Spence."

"Who is it?"

Pause. "Ellie, your goal is to matchmake Candy, not me."

A pause could only mean one thing….

"Sara Montgomery, you wanton mortgage broker you. You landed a guy! While sitting *alone* at the beach house! You rule."

Sara laughed and signed off.

Ellie shook her head. And here she'd been pondering how to help Sara relax, have some fun. Appeared Sara was a lot more resourceful than Ellie had given her credit for.

She started to slip her cell into her shorts' pocket, hesitated, then punched in the speed-dial for Dark Gothic Roast. Overhead, seagulls squawked and circled as a little boy tossed pieces of bread from a bag. Nearby, construction workers hammered, drilled, called out to each other as they worked on the festival site.

"Dark Gothic Roast," answered a female voice.

"Hey!" yelled a male voice. "That your Benz?"

Ellie looked around. "Tish, El. How's it going?"

A groan. "Kiefer called in sick and I ended up handling the morning rush by myself."

"Hey," boomed the male voice again. "I'm talking to you. Miss Spiky Black Hair."

As if that left any doubt who he meant. As Tish droned on about the espresso machine making a "funny sound," Ellie scanned the area. None of the construction workers seemed interested in her. Nor did the nearby jocks tossing a Frisbee.

Wait.

There.

The guy in the Hawaiian shirt, unbuttoned to reveal a buffed, brown and extremely hairy chest, was staring directly at her.

"It sounds kind of like keee-keee klunk," continued Tish, "and it only does it if I'm steaming milk longer than twenty seconds...."

Ellie stared at the man. Something about him looked familiar.

"I suppose I could stop steaming sooner," said Tish, "but then there'd be no froth and you know how some customers would get if their lattes were flat...."

The man smiled, and Ellie's heart ratcheted in her chest.

Only one man in the world had a smile like that.

Impossible...and yet...it was him.

Bill Romero.

He was older—seventeen years to be exact—bigger and *hotter* than the boy she remembered. The rough-around-the-edges guy had morphed into a body like The Rock, with the too-cool aura of a Lenny Kravitz. He leaned against a palm tree, the breezes billowing open his shirt whose bright yellow flowers looked like pats of melting butter on his choca-mocha-latte skin.

"El, what should I do about the espresso machine?"

Ellie cleared her suddenly parched throat. "Turn up the steam," she rasped before terminating the call.

"That your Benz?" he called out again.

Ah, the voice. It hadn't really changed. That deep, rumbling tone and clipped rhythm, so familiar it made her insides squeeze. How many nights had she lain in her childhood bed, her window open on the off chance she'd overhear Bill talking with a pal or family member. The summer she turned twelve, when he was eighteen, she must have written more journals than Anais Nin. Page after page filled with fantasies of her first kiss—her first everything—with him.

"Benz," he repeated, mistaking her silence for not hearing him clearly. "Over there!" He pointed.

Ellie stared at his raised arm. So big, so brown, two-thirds of it covered with a massive tattoo. She couldn't really see the details this far away, but could tell it was colorful, bold and elaborate.

Unlike her tattoos, which were hidden, secretive.

Sea breezes brushed and stroked her, making her realize all the areas of her skin that were bare. In the distance, she heard waves crashing, the fading away of a girl's laughter.

Finally remembering to breathe, Ellie looked to where he was pointing. At the far end of the patch of tarmac sat a gleaming silver Mercedes. She had the momentary urge to laugh—did she really look like the kind of woman who drove a *Benz?* She looked back at him, wondering if, behind those dark shades, his eyes still looked like melted pools of chocolate.

"No," she called out, her voice breathy, unrecognizable. "Not mine."

He pushed himself off the palm tree—did his biceps ripple when he moved?—and stared at her. The sun glinted off an earring. That was new, too. And for a crazy moment, she wondered if he remembered her. No, no way. Back then, she'd been freckled and mousy-haired. Hardly the goth chick he was talking to right now.

Besides, they'd only really spoken once, that memorable summer night she'd worked up the nerve to ask if what she'd heard was true, was he was really moving far away? Her girl's heart had shattered into a million pieces when he'd said yes, he was moving to New York to start film school.

"Just my luck," he murmured, his voice rippling through the air like a heat wave. "Need it moved, hoped it might be yours."

She wiped a trickle of sweat off her brow, wishing she could say something, anything, to prolong this encounter. She was a whiz at chatting, did it all the time with her customers. Asked them about their jobs, their kids. Helped them figure out their love problems. But she couldn't summon one reasonably intelligent thing to ask Bill. Yeah, good ol' helpful Ellie was resourceful when it came to others' needs, but a tongue-tied, sweat-laden mass of messed-up hormones when it came to her own.

She took a few halting steps across the sand, imagining how she'd introduce herself. "Hey, remember me? That scrawny kid next door who wore pigtails?" No, skip the scrawny part. "The girl next door who…" loved, adored, idolized you. No, forget that. Although Bill had been a few years older than Matt, he'd probably remember her brother. Yeah, she'd bring up Matt. "Hey, remember me? Matt Rockwell's kid sister?"

She stopped.

Too late.

Bill was talking to several women, one dressed in Benz-worthy clothes, undoubtedly wicked and cool. And flirting unabashedly with Bill. Jeez, her effusive giggle could be heard over the construction workers' incessant hammering, even over a low-flying airplane towing a bright blue banner with the words Wolfman Pizza 1-800-555-9844 We're Howling Good!

And I've howlingly lost my chance.

She stopped, stared down at her purple-painted toenails, white legs, black shorts, black silk top. Then back up at the giggling babe with the white short-shorts, long bronzed legs and skimpy pink halter top.

They obviously weren't talking about the Benz or she'd be moving it.

I'm standing here, looking like a black dot in the middle of the sand. The anti-beach babe. The kind of woman he'd ask to move her car, but nothing more.

With a sinking feeling, Ellie turned and started heading back to the beach house. It was for the best. She needed to see how Candy and Matt were doing. Catch the story about Sara and this mystery male. Follow up with Tish, make sure the espresso machine wasn't getting the better of her. What had she said it sounded like? *Keee-keee klunk?*

Funny, that's exactly how Ellie felt at the moment. As though something inside her had jarred loose and was rattling around. And she knew what that something was. A piece of her past named Bill. And here she was, walking away for a second time from him, just as she had that long-ago summer night when she was twelve.

Seventeen years and hundreds of life changes later, walking away today felt every bit as hard.

THREE HOURS, two Bomb Pops and one Candy-Sara-Ellie girl-talk fest later, Ellie stood in the cosmetics aisle at Walgreens with Sara, perusing the hair color section.

"I can't believe I agreed to be made over into a beach babe," muttered Ellie, looking at the boxes of color with names like Bombshell Blond, Golden Sunset and Strawberry Vanilla.

Sara, switching their plastic shopping basket from one hand to the other, snorted a laugh. "Gotta look like one if you want to wow them at the audition tomorrow morning. Plus, if—no, *when*—you get hired, think of all those points Team Java Mammas will get toward the grand prize!"

Team Java Mammas. The team name she, Candy and Sara had given themselves in their quest to win the festival grand prize, a free beach bungalow rental every summer for the next ten years. "Just wish I could wow them with black spiky hair," Ellie muttered.

"I'll pretend I didn't hear that." Sara scanned the boxes, all decorated with smiling models sporting luxurious, shiny hair in more shades than a color wheel.

For a surreal moment, everything looked too light, too blond, too perfect. Too anti-Ellie. What was she doing here? Not just here at the store, but here at the beach, too! She wasn't some sixteen-year-old starring in Beach Blanket Babettes—she was a businesswoman turning *thirty* in a few months! She shouldn't be here. She should be back at Dark Gothic Roast, getting ready for the big move.

"I don't know, Sara—" she gestured toward the sea of models' faces "—I'll never look like them."

"Hon, even *they* don't look like that. They've been airbrushed and streamlined and photo-enhanced down to their very roots."

It wasn't the words as much as the lilt in her pal's voice that shook Ellie out of her funk. She looked at Sara more closely, realizing her telltale lines of stress had all but disappeared. As corny as it sounded, she even had a *twinkle* in her eye.

And Ellie knew why. She'd just forgotten why's name.

"What was that surfer hunk's name?"

"Drew." The way Sara said his name, it sounded like a piece of delectable candy. "And yours…"

Mine. Oh, man, that was *so* far from the truth.

"Bill." Ellie heaved a small sigh. Crazy how just saying his name sent small shivers all over her. And to think she'd just told herself she wasn't some goofy sixteen-year-old. Truth was, saying his name turned her insides all gooey, like some besotted, crushed-out teenager.

"How long were you two neighbors?"

"Years. I remember first seeing him when I was six, the year my dad left. Bill was twelve, and already a stud-in-the-making."

"You had a crush on him at *six?*"

Ellie nodded slowly. "Crazy, huh? I still remember the first time I saw him. He was standing on his porch, staring out at nothing, lost in thought. I thought he looked like a fairy-tale prince. After that, my heart did a sonic boom every time I saw him, right up to the day he moved to New York to go to film school."

"How old were you when he moved?"

"Twelve."

"You must have been so sad."

"Sad? That was the year the movie *When Harry Met Sally* came out. I saw it at least ten times. I'd sit in the back, drowning my sorrow in popcorn, fantasizing about Bill and how, despite our tumultuous parting, we were destined to be together." She pointed at the box Sara was holding. "Honey blond, no way."

"But, El—"

"Too Reese Witherspoon. I need a bad-girl blond color."

"No, I meant…" Sara hesitated, then set the box back on the shelf. "I was still feeling sad about your childhood heartache."

Ellie didn't want to admit some of that sadness had come back today. She couldn't blame Bill for not recognizing her, but something about his lack of attention had made her feel again like that broken-hearted twelve-year-old.

"So," said Sara, "what's a bad-girl blond? The color of Madonna's hair?"

Ellie felt relieved to be back on topic. "She's not so bad anymore, is she?"

"Cameron Diaz?"

"Maybe."

"Jennifer Aniston?"

Elle gave her friend a look. "Girlfriend, you need to unchain yourself more often from that laptop because obviously you have *no* idea what bad is."

They laughed.

"El," Sara said, turning serious, "I know you're not the type to easily talk about what's on your heart, but I have to add one thing. Maybe it wasn't a coincidence that you saw Bill today. I bet you're going to run into him again."

See Bill *again?* Ellie didn't know if her heart, mind or soul could handle it. What had happened this morning was enough to haunt her for months as it was. But no way did she want Sara to know that. Ellie Rockwell was so much better than some ancient crushed-out angst.

She hoped.

"As much as I've always wanted to have a real supernatural experience," she said in her best breezy voice, "I doubt you've suddenly turned clairvoyant."

Before Sara could follow up with something else serious and heartfelt, Ellie pointed toward the end of the aisle. "Hey, down there are some awesome black hair colors."

Sara made a stopping gesture. "You promised to go blond, and I'm holding you to it. This one—" she grabbed a hair color labeled Lightning Blond "—is perfect. After we wash out your black rinse, this color will give you that Gwen Stefani bad-girl blond you want."

"Okay, we're starting to talk bad."

Grinning, Sara picked up a second container. "Then we'll add some gold highlights, which will give you that sunny, sparkling beach babe look."

Ellie looked over at a couple of sunny, sparkling beachettes. The type who'd snagged Bill's attention today. Here she thought she'd so smoothly avoided further discussion of Bill, but she'd forgotten the nonstop banter in her own head.

One of the beachettes laughed, reminding her of the bimbo Bill had chortled with earlier today. What did those types have that Ellie didn't? Hell, if she could make herself over into the Mistress of the

Dark, she could certainly make herself into a Gidget type, too. Not the sunny, sparkling variety, but definitely a Gidget on the Edge.

"Bad-girl with gold streaks it is," she said, turning back to Sara. "Sold."

"That's my girl! Hey, El, this is fun taking care of you for a change. Oh, look at these yummy pastel lipsticks…"

"Huhhhh." Blond was one thing, but *pastel* make-up?

Sara tossed a peachy lipstick into the basket. "I told you I bought several new bikinis for the trip, right? We're about the same size, so let's have you try a few on when we get back."

"What colors are they?" Not pastel, please God.

"Pink, tangerine…oh, and black."

Ellie's mood lifted. "Black. Cool."

"Okay, next—spray-on tan."

This time Ellie willingly followed her friend to the fake bake aisle, as Sara called it.

Sara held up something called TechnoTan. "What about—"

"Put it in, baby."

Sara, looking surprised but pleased, added it to the basket. "I won't spray over your tattoos, but use one of my makeup brushes to paint the skin around them."

Ellie listened, sort of, but her attention had again been diverted by the beachettes who were giggling in front of the body cream section. It brought back how she'd felt earlier, Miss Black Spiked Hair Can You Move Your Benz, standing in the background, out of place and out of time, wearing her big, broken childhood heart on her sleeve. Okay, so she'd wanted to be better than ancient angst, but the truth was, she wasn't.

Suddenly, it felt as though all the years of caring and yearning and dreaming about Bill had crowded against her heart, squeezing it, constricting the memories into a throbbing lump of ache. Today, her world had stopped when she'd recognized Bill, but his didn't even pause. *He wasn't interested in me.* And as much as she told herself it didn't matter, she felt rejected. Unacceptable.

She picked up a box of something and pretended to read, as though focusing on random words might impose logic on her pain. On her heart. But the letters danced and swam, refusing to make sense.

Maybe that's how she should view the past. Make it blurry, indistinguishable, unimportant. Do what she came to do this week—chill, play matchmaker, audition to be an extra and screw the rest.

"Hey!" enthused Sara, holding up a plastic case. "This will look fantastic with your turquoise eyes. Ghost Silver eye shadow!"

Ghost...exactly how she should view Bill. A ghost from her past, nothing more.

She took the container from Ellie and tossed it into the basket. "Sold."

2

BILL, SITTING in the first row of the audience, shook his head at Mandy, the hyperefficient fortyish principal casting director sitting at the foot of the stage. She nodded, understanding his message that the girl who just auditioned was a no.

"You didn't like her?" asked Jimmie, Bill's best pal and *Sin on the Beach*'s key grip.

"Not hot enough," Bill said, shifting. He tipped his coffee mug, which caused brown liquid to slosh down the front of his white polo shirt.

"Shit."

He set the cup on the sand beneath their folding chairs and pulled the shirt away from his skin. "I'm used to easing into Monday mornings with 9:00 a.m. read-throughs, not getting up when the rooster crows to audition hundreds of extras for some publicity gig." He flapped the shirt to cool the spilled liquid.

"I won't ask if *that* was hot enough," quipped Jimmie.

Bill shot him a look.

"Sorry. But speaking of things that *could* be

hot...have you given any more thought to you and I starting our own indie company?"

Bill nodded. "Sure. Problem is, making big bucks with an independent film production company is a long shot."

"Who's talking big bucks?"

"Me. You know my take on the movie business. Dream big, make it big. No offense, but an indie company is too small for this boy."

Jimmie shook his head. "You're letting your hard-luck roots get the better of you, pal. Producing our own films gives us control, which is big in a better way. Did I tell you *Edge of the Universe* placed first in its category at the WorldFest competition?"

He and Jimmie had known each other from their first day at New York University film school, given each other a lot of support while they crawled up the dog-eat-dog success ladder of L.A. film and television work. Jimmie's first love was screenwriting, but until he started making sales, he worked on film crews.

Bill balled his hand into a fist, knocked it against Jimmie's fist. "*Edge of the Universe* will be your breakthrough sale, no doubt about it."

Jimmie had spent the last few years writing this screenplay, about three friends from East L.A. whose lives take dramatically different paths. He'd loosely based the protagonist on Bill's own coming of age story in East L.A.'s gangland. Bill hadn't minded sharing most aspects of what it'd been like growing up in the barrio but there was one thing he never shared with anyone, and never would.

"It could be our first script, Bill. With a hot screenwriter and a hot up-and-coming director…" He jabbed his thumb at himself, Bill. "My parents are willing to be our first investors, although we'd need to raise the rest. I think we can do it."

Bill paused. "You're my best friend, Jimmie, but I gotta say no. It took years to nail this first AD spot. Gordon's still the director on this week's shoot, but he's stepping aside and letting me take the reins for a few days. If I pull it off, I'll be bagging my first directing gig with *Sin*."

First AD—Assistant Director—was the number two spot on the set, right below director. As such, Bill was basically the jack-of-all-trades on the set, but that wasn't good enough. He wanted to call the shots, be number one. Being the oldest of five kids, as well the man of the house after his dad split, Bill had decided early on that the world belonged to those who stayed strong and focused.

And his focus was to make his mark as a film director.

Which meant he said no to anything that got in his way, even his best pal's business idea.

"Look," he said, lowering his voice, "if I hear of anyone wanting to start up an indie, I'll put them in touch with you, okay?"

"Not that I don't appreciate that, but my first choice will always be you."

Bill groaned. "Is this the part where I say 'We'll always have Paris'?"

Jimmie laughed, gave his pal a friendly slap on the back. "I'll stop laying on the guilt. Besides, you have better things to do. Do you know how many guys would *kill* to fill in for the director on a cattle call for babes in bikinis?"

Bill caught Mandy's wave. Next audition was ready.

"Yeah, it's a burden, but somebody's gotta do it."

He gave a go-ahead nod to Mandy, a small gesture toward a big career. People like Jim just didn't get it.

IN THE BACKSTAGE TENT provided for those auditioning to be extras, Ellie checked herself out in a mirror, amazed yet again at her transformation from a goth chick to this bad-girl blonde in a good-time bikini. Most of it thanks to Sara, who'd woken Ellie up at the crack of dawn and helped wrangle her into beach babe shape.

Ellie looked around at the other extra wannabes hanging out in the small blue tent. They'd all shown up at 7:00 a.m. to sign up, and in the hour since, they'd spent their time primping, talking and drinking the free coffee from one of several urns. Free, but disgustingly *bad*-tasting coffee, although no one except Ellie seemed to notice.

Which was the only bad thing—besides her bad-girl blond hair—about this whole adventure. Now that she was here, she was psyched to audition. It felt silly but fun to try out for a walk-on part on *Sin on the Beach*. And although it felt a little odd, it was nice to do something for herself instead of everybody else.

"Ellie Rockwell?" asked a harried teenage boy wearing a *Sin on the Beach* festival T-shirt and khaki shorts. He looked around the tent while speaking in low tones into his headset.

"Yes?"

"You're next. Follow me." He hurried away, reporting his movements to whoever was on the other end of the headset. "She's here. Yes. Ellie Rockwell. Maybe."

Maybe? What did that mean?

He held open the flap to the tent for Ellie to follow. She grabbed her bag of makeup in one hand, her bag containing her killer stilettos in the other, and followed.

They sprinted across a patch of hot sand and into another tent, this one huge, white and air-conditioned. Ellie paused, relishing the blast of cool air. The area was buzzing with people, props, equipment. In the far corner, next to a table set with rolls, fruit and drinks, a man sporting a handlebar mustache, lime-green turban and a gaudy Hawaiian shirt was pouring himself a big glass of iced tea. He looked up at Ellie and winked.

Oh, hold me back.

"You're up," the boy said, motioning toward an opening in the tent. "Walk onto the stage, head to the microphone and answer their questions. Afterward, exit stage left."

"Who's they?"

"Assistant director, casting director, maybe one of the producers."

Her stomach flip-flopped. These were the big-wigs, the muckety-mucks, the top dogs who ran her favorite show. Okay, sitting with all the extra wanna-bes, it had been easy to think this was fun and silly. But knowing who she'd be auditioning in front of, suddenly this felt freaking scary.

"Stage left?" she rasped, kicking off her sandals. She cleared her throat. "Where's that?"

"The far side of the stage."

She slipped on a stiletto. "Did you say there's a *microphone?*"

But he was already engrossed in another conversation over his headset. Catching Ellie's gaze, he impatiently pointed toward the stage and mouthed an emphatic "Go!" before zipping away.

She quickly stepped into the second stiletto, trying to ignore the little voice in her head telling her to run away, she'd only make a fool of herself, people might laugh, she could fall on her face....

Straightening, she sucked in a shaky breath. *If I can't tackle one silly audition, how do I expect to tackle a new business venture?*

She walked onto the stage.

BILL WATCHED the next girl walk hesitantly out onto the stage. She walked stiff-kneed, staring wide-eyed at the audience that was mostly made up of friends of those auditioning, some crew, a few hungover partiers. When she reached the microphone, she stopped and smiled awkwardly.

She was pretty, in a Kirsten Dunst kind of way, with her short, fluffy blond hair, dimpled smile and pert nose. The kind of girl one saw a hundred times a day in L.A.

And yet…not.

Something about her was different, but he couldn't put his finger on it. Something provocative, simmering just below the surface…

"Look at those *shoes,* man," muttered Jimmie, sitting taller in his seat.

Bill's gaze dropped down the nicely filled black bikini, down long, coltish legs to a pair of black patent stilettos with silver chains. *Whoa.* That something different was hardly below the surface, it was just below the shapely calves.

"Tell us your name, where you're from and something special about yourself," prompted Peter, the casting assistant in charge of extras, into his hand-held mike. Nearby sat Mandy, talking on her cell phone while eating a doughnut.

The young woman leaned forward, at which point Bill noticed the edge of a tattoo peeking over the top of her bikini top. A spiderweb?

She spoke so closely to the mike, it sounded like a thunderous whisper. "Ellie Rockwell."

"Step back and say your name again, please," instructed Peter.

She did. Bill liked the cadence of her voice. Soft, rhythmic like the waves.

And familiar.

She shifted from one spiked heel to the other. "I'm an L.A. girl—grew up in East L.A., currently living and working in West L.A."

A sense of déjà vu prickled his skin. He knew her. But from where? With the long hours he put in on the set these days, his only social outlet was Gold's Gym, and he'd have recalled if their paths had crossed there. Maybe it was her voice, someone he'd conversed with in the course of his too-many business calls every day.

Wait a minute.

Rockwell?

East L.A.?

Hadn't he had neighbors there, years ago, with that name? Right, now he remembered. Mrs. Rockwell, one of those fragile blondes who looked as though she'd crumble if you looked at her the wrong way, and her kids Mark—no, Matt—and a daughter. Yeah, had to be Ellie. He blew out a puff of air. That freckled, knobby-kneed girl had grown up to be this dom-shoed doll on the stage?

"Four stars," murmured Jimmie.

But ever since Jimmie tied the knot last year, he'd been irritatingly intent on setting Bill up for wedded bliss, too. Every potential Mrs. Romero got a star-rating from one—forget it—to four—go for it.

"You and your damn numbers," Bill muttered,

tapping the pencil against his clipboard. But four was dead-on as his gaze raked up past that cleavage-spilling black top to that heart-shaped face to those eyes....

He flashed on a memory from years ago. Ellie, auburn hair barely restrained in pigtails, those big questioning eyes. It had been long past midnight. He'd been sitting on the porch, contemplating his life changes to come, when suddenly he looked down and saw his young neighbor standing on the lawn in front of him. In a soft voice, she'd asked if what she'd heard was true—was he moving to New York?

She'd sounded so anxious, so sad, which had confused him. But with younger siblings, he knew how a kid's unresolved worries could be triggered by a seemingly unrelated event. If he remembered correctly, Ellie's dad had split around this time five or so years before. Another adult figure leaving probably reminded her of that all over again.

Bill had answered her yes, he was moving to New York to go to film school, and that little girls shouldn't be out so late. He'd walked her back to her house where she'd lingered in the front doorway, those big eyes staring at him, before going inside.

Those same eyes stared at him now, reeling him back to the present, and he offered a small smile of recognition. She smiled back, and he swore something in her look shifted, darkened, sparked. For a long moment, they held each other's gaze and suddenly all he was aware of was a churning tension between them, not unlike the distant crashing waves.

He'd at first observed a woman in a black bikini, but now all he saw were glistening limbs, full breasts, bare skin. Lust had fogged his brain and whatever memories he had of the girl evaporated, replaced by this hot woman.

Jimmie coughed. "Five."

"Five what?"

"That eye-lock, as though you two are the only people in this place, just bumped her from four to five stars."

"You've never given a five."

"Yeah, well, I've never seen you go brain-dead so quickly, either."

Bill broke the eye-lock and glanced at his buddy. "It's an *audition,* Jimbo, nothing more."

"Bill-o, sell *that* bridge somewhere else."

Peter lit a cigarette, blowing out a puff of smoke as he said into his mike, "You have one minute to share something special about yourself."

Ellie blinked, straightened, released a shaky breath. Over the speakers, the sound reverberated over the crowd like a throaty sigh, nearly bringing Bill to his knees.

She zeroed in on him again. Later, he pondered if he'd imagined the look she gave him, one filled with a yearning that bordered on defiance. But he didn't imagine her next words.

"I want to share this with you."

Slowly, she turned so her back was to the audience. God. Those heels worked magic on a great ass and a pair of killer legs.

"You're gnawing on your pencil," whispered Jimmie.

Bill released the eraser tip from his teeth. "Oh, shut up."

Ellie slipped her thumbs underneath the waist-band of her bikini bottoms and lowered them, slowly, an inch or so. Bill ground his teeth, his entire body on edge, as he read the black-scripted tattoo at the base of her spine.

"Queen of Evil?" he rasped.

"Yeah," murmured Jimmie, "that's what it says all right."

Bill groaned.

Jimmie leaned closer. "So, is she a five?"

Bill returned his gaze to her, gave his head a slow shake. "She's more than a number, Jimmie. I share a past with her."

"Ellie Rockwell."

Standing at the food table in the backstage tent quaffing a blueberry muffin, she froze. Even with her back to him, she'd know that voice anywhere. Swallowing her bite, she set down the muffin and turned.

A shiver passed through her.

Bill was even hotter up close.

His skin, naturally mocha, was darker from the sun. His full, natural hair looked like a deliciously dark aura. Stubble coarsened his jaw, making her think he'd probably rolled out of bed and come straight here for today's audition without shaving. She shouldn't have thought about him rolling out of bed, because she started wondering if he was one of those men who slept in his shorts or pajama bottoms.

Or naked.

She sucked in a shaky breath. *He's only said my name and I already have him naked in bed.*

A hint of a smile raised a corner of his mouth. She hadn't noticed before that he sported a soul patch, neatly trimmed, underneath his full bottom lip.

"Ellie Rockwell, right?"

"Bill Romero," she whispered, then cleared her throat. "I saw you in the audience."

"I thought you noticed me." He looked her up and down. "You've...changed."

"You don't know the half of it," she murmured, her gaze sliding down to the colorful tattoo that trailed from underneath his sleeve down to his elbow. Appeared to be the tail of something.

"It's a dragon," he explained.

Her gaze traveled back up the green and burnished gold scales that disappeared underneath his sleeve.

"The rest," he murmured, "goes up my arm. One claw's on my back, and its head falls across my chest."

She stared at his chest, imagining the head of the beast permanently inked on his molded pec.

"A fire-breathing, ice-breathing or acid-spitting dragon?"

"Fire." He looked surprised. "No one's ever asked me that before."

Being a good glam goth chick, she knew her dragon basics, but no way she'd admit that. Usually her attitude was if somebody didn't like her style, tough. But this was different. This was Bill Romero. He'd obviously come backstage to see the beach babe Ellie, and no way she'd let on he'd fallen for a look that was the antithesis of the real her. This was Cinderella at the ball time. The prince was flirting with her, and she was going to run with it.

"I think I saw some of those dragons when I got my Queen of Evil tattoo," she lied.

Bill made a murmur of approval. "Now *that's* a tattoo I'd like to hear more about." He glanced over her shoulder at the half-eaten muffin. "Looks like I interrupted your snack?"

She made a dismissive gesture toward it. "I'd skipped breakfast, so…"

"I skipped breakfast, too." His gaze held hers for a moment. "If I didn't have to get back, I'd suggest we grab a bite. Catch up."

Get back? She flashed back to yesterday when he'd asked if that was her car. He hadn't been dressed up either day…could he be making money parking cars? She wouldn't ask, didn't want to embarrass him. What had happened to his dreams?

"Last we saw each other," she said nonchalantly, "you were leaving for film school."

"Yeah, went to New York University." He cocked that half smile again. "Surprised you remember."

She shrugged as though, oh, sure, just one of those things that popped up from some distant memory instead of something she'd thought about a lot these past seventeen years. Everything about that night he'd told her he was moving away was burned indelibly into her brain. The moon had been full, yellow and waxy in a smoggy sky. Lavender scented the air. Down the block a radio blasted a popular Ice-T rap song.

She waited for Bill to say more, but nothing. Had he come back to L.A., armed with his degree, only to find nobody wanted to hire another starry-eyed wannabe? She'd seen a lot of people lose their dreams in the city of dreams. Actresses who thought they'd be the next Meryl Streep, writers who thought they'd be the next Eszterhas, directors who thought they'd be the next Scorsese. All of them waiting for their big breaks while serving tables or working on construction sites or...

Parking cars.

She dropped her gaze, caught the splatter of brown on his shirt. "Spill something?"

He looked down, back up with a sheepish smile. "Coffee. Actually, I took a break from my casting duties to see if I can get it out. My buddy's covering for me."

She blinked. "Casting duties?"

"Yeah." He raked a hand through his thick, full hair. "I'm just helping out, for today only."

"Part-time job?"

"More like a favor."

So things hadn't gone well. She'd get off the topic, help him save face. "I'd suggest dabbing that with soda water. If you can't find that, cold water." She smiled. "I run a coffee shop so I deal with stuff like this all the time."

"Coffee shop, eh? I'll definitely take your advice, then." But he didn't do a thing except stand there and stare at her. Was her bad-girl blonde makeover working?

"I should be getting back," he murmured.

"Sure." *Do something! Invite him to the beach house, ask him out for another cup of coffee to make up for the one he sloshed, ask his zodiac sign,* something. "Nice seeing you." *Good one, El. Your big moment and you wuss out.*

"Nice seeing you, too." He started walking away, paused. "Going to the festival later?"

"I'm entering some of the events. My girlfriends and I want to win the grand prize. You can enter as a group, you know, so that's what we're doing." *I'm babbling.* "Except for this audition. Not a group thing, obviously. We figured after I was done over as a beach babe…" *Not good. Overbabble.*

"Done over?"

She smiled shakily. "Girl talk for getting fixed up." She'd never lied this much. "I probably wouldn't have auditioned if they hadn't made me do it." At least that was the truth.

He looked her down, back up, making a zillion goose pimples skitter across her skin.

"I'm an idiot," he mumbled. He hit the palm of his hand against his forehead. "I got so caught up seeing you again, I forgot to tell you something." He smiled warmly. "It's a good thing your girlfriends talked you into auditioning, because Ellie Rockwell, you're hired."

She blinked. "I am?"

He nodded.

"*You* get to pick people?"

"Just for today. See Peter, the casting assistant who's sitting in the front row, and tell him I said you're hired. He'll explain how you're paid, where to report, stuff like that."

"Great. Thanks."

They stared at each other for another long moment.

"I need to get out there," Bill finally said.

"Right. You don't want to blow this opportunity."

He frowned.

She gestured lamely toward the audience out there. "You know, doing this casting gig you're doing as a favor could lead to another job."

He looked surprised, then sputtered a laugh. "I already have a job on *Sin on the Beach*. I'm the first assistant director."

Her body felt as though a shock wave had passed through it. Not unlike how she'd felt years ago at a high-decibel, sensory-overload Marilyn Manson concert. Bill wasn't some dreamy-eyed wannabe, he was the first assistant *director*. Of *Sin on the Beach*.

A Big Man on the Set. He probably had bikini-clad chicky-babes hanging all over him 24/7.

So what if he came backstage to tell her she was hired, tell her he remembered her, there was no way such a hotshot would want anything more to do with an extra.

Bill scrubbed his knuckle over his chin. "A lot of those festival competitions require two people to compete."

She nodded.

"Might be a little awkward to enter some of those with your girlfriends...unless you're into that sort of thing."

It took her a moment to get his drift.

"You think I'm— Oh, no." She laughed at the thought of her being lesbo with Candy or Sara. "Not that they aren't attractive and fascinating women, but I'm not into that. Anyway, they both appear to have guys they're entering the contests with."

"And you don't?"

"No."

"How terrible." He gave her a look that made her kneecaps go soft.

"Yes," she murmured, "downright horrible."

He grinned, glanced at his watch. "After auditions, I'll have the rest of the day off. Meet me backstage, same spot, at two o'clock and I'll be your partner."

It took a moment for the adrenaline rush to subside before she remembered how to nod yes. *Partner.* That had to be on par with "date," right?

She was having a date with Bill Romero.

Bill take-my-heart-and-do-me-all-night-long Romero.

As long as she got home before her carriage turned into a pumpkin, and her bikini into her glam goth T-shirt, this could be a fairy-tale date to die for.

"Two it is," she whispered.

3

ELLIE WAS TOO PUNCTUAL for her own good. Not that being on time was a bad thing, but it was when you were overly anxious to see the guy of your childhood dreams, who happened to *not* be punctual. Backstage again at the food table, she nibbled on grapes and hoped she looked okay in her red bikini, fishnet cover-up, retro polka-dot wedgies and over-the-shoulder mini brocade purse. When she'd left the beach house, she'd felt fine, but after passing dozens of girls in Easter-egg color bikinis and nondescript sandals, she was starting to wonder if she looked too over-the-top.

That she, a glam goth diva, was actually *fretting* about looking over-the-top suddenly made her laugh. Back at her apartment, her entire wardrobe was a swirl of purple, black and red satins and laces. This beach babe makeover was frying her brain. Next she'd be buying frosted pink lipstick, eating granola and saying "dude."

"Hey, how's my Ellie?" said a familiar, deep voice. Bill.

Her heart thumped a wanton, pagan beat.

My Ellie. She lost the ability to speak for a moment. "Great." *My Bill.*

He looked effing incredible. That mocha skin, those brown eyes, that windblown black 'fro—colors so rich and dark, they made her insides quiver.

Maybe it was because of the canvas tent, but the light seemed pale and ephemeral. Summer heat shimmered in the air, hot and intangible. And in the midst of it all stood Bill, like a chocolatey, rough-edged hip-hop prince. Wild on the outside, in control on the inside.

The moment was broken when a girl, who looked to be around nineteen, bounded up and tapped Bill on the arm. She wore short-shorts, a halter top, her shiny blond hair tied back in a ponytail. Daisy Mae's long-lost twin, no doubt.

The girl looked up at Bill with round liquid-blue eyes and smiled.

"Curtiss is having some problems with the boom mike for tomorrow morning's shoot," she said in a baby-doll voice. "He wanted me to tell you he's picking up a new one today as backup."

"Thanks." Bill nodded, turned his attention back to Ellie.

But Daisy Baby-Doll didn't leave. "I'm the new PA. Name's Phoebe."

Bill looked at her. "Hi, Phoebe."

"Actually, my name's Diane, but that's so boring, so a few years ago I started calling myself Phoebe, and now everybody remembers me!"

Ellie had a feeling she knew why.

"Well, Phoebe," said Bill, "nice meeting you—"

"If you ever need anything…" she said, her voice trailing off.

Like it was so hard to guess what that *anything* might be. To stop herself from saying something she might regret, Ellie stuffed a grape into her mouth.

Of course, women had always loved Bill, and he'd loved his share back. She had many memories watching him from her living room window while he laughed and flirted with the girls on the block. Even back then, he had that certain something that attracted the opposite sex in droves. Call it confidence, charm or being blessed with more than his share of pheromones, but the guy had *it*.

Bill glanced at Ellie, back to Phoebe. "Look, I'm taking a meeting here…."

Taking a meeting? This wasn't a date? Ellie shoved another grape in her mouth.

Phoebe rolled back her shoulders, which made her breasts stick out even more, and plastered on a smile. "Well, Bill, see you around the set."

She'd barely bounced away before a tall, preppie-looking guy sidled up to Bill. "Man, you should be bottled."

"Behave." Bill turned to Ellie. "This is my main man, Jimmie," he said. "We met on our first day at NYU. I was the tough guy from East L.A. Jimmie was the class act from Connecticut. I decided to like him anyway."

She smiled while swallowing the grape, which felt like a chunk of lead going down her throat. "Nice to meet you, Jimmie."

"This is Ellie Belle," said Bill. He slung his arm around his friend's shoulders. "He taught me how to order wine, and I taught him how to siphon gas."

But she was still back at Ellie Belle. Nobody had called her that in years. It had been her dad's nickname for her, one her mom had occasionally used after her dad left, but nobody had used it since. Not even Matt. Had Bill overheard one of her parents and, all these years later, remembered?

Jimmie extended his hand, which she took. "And after that eloquent introduction, let me say it's very nice to meet you."

"Nice to meet you, too." They shook hands.

"Heard you two were next-door neighbors years ago."

"That's right."

"No offense, but you sure don't look like someone from the hood."

"Well, we don't normally wear bikinis with fishnet cover-ups there."

Jimmie looked surprised, then laughed. "I, uh, didn't mean that."

"Sorry, I knew what you meant." She'd heard comments like that plenty of times, mostly from people who'd rarely, if ever, been to the hood. She used to take offense, then realized what mattered more than a person's question was the intention behind it. Jimmie, despite his Brooks Brothers appearance and precise diction, had a sincere streak.

"Actually, when my mom and her mother moved there in the late fifties, there were families in that neighborhood straight out of *Father Knows Best*. The melting pot started getting stirred more during the seventies." She'd skip over what everyone knew—that the area grew economically depressed, gangs arrived, street crime mushroomed and that's when things could get dicey if you didn't already have your friends and community in place, which the Rockwells did. "The hood's changing for the better these days, though."

Bill made a disgruntled noise.

"It's true. Homes are being renovated, new businesses are moving in—"

"C'mon, Ellie, nobody *really* cares about our old stomping ground. The powers that be wrote off that part of L.A. a long time ago. I, for one, will never go back."

"Can't turn your back on your roots," Jimmie said to Bill. "Don't you still have family there?"

"Those who stayed deserved what they got."

Ellie bit the inside of her lip. She didn't like hearing his negativity, but she had to remember how Bill, like Matt, had taken on the role of man of the house at an early age. Except Bill had had four younger siblings, which hadn't been easy.

Jimmie, obviously picking up on the heavy vibes, changed the subject. "Those are some shoes." He nudged his head toward her feet.

"They're retro sling back wedgies," she said,

tipping the toe of red-and-white polka-dot sandals this way, then that. "Got them at Sinister Shoes."

Bill gave her a funny look. "Sinister Shoes?"

"I've heard of that place," said Jimmie. "It's down on Melrose. All the goths go there to shop."

"Goths." Bill shook his head. "Elvira's cool, but I don't get that whole vampire thing. They all seem depressed or something."

Her insides shrank a little. Made her feel like a fake and a liar pretending not to be one of those into *that whole vampire thing*. It was really about loving the darkness, the mystery in life, but she didn't want to explain.

All she wanted was this day, this experience with Bill, and for that she was willing to pretend she was somebody she wasn't.

She angled her leg, showing off. "These shoes are really more of a retro pinup look," she said a little too gaily. "Similar to what Betty Grable wore in those World War II posters."

Bill and Jimmie stared at her.

"Betty Grable?" Bill finally said. "She was a movie star *way* before your time."

"I've always loved the Golden Age of Hollywood, even as a little kid. I sometimes envision the stars like Audrey Hepburn, Veronica Lake, Betty Grable when I design some of my clothes." When they looked at her black fishnet cover-up over her red bikini, she added drolly, "These aren't my designs. I bought them at Target."

A grin sauntered across Bill's lips. "You did a lot of sewing as a kid, didn't you? I think my mom said something about it once."

She nodded, feeling a little giddy that he'd remembered something else about her as a child. Maybe she'd been more memorable than she'd given herself credit for.

"Hollywood's Golden Era is one of my favorites," he continued. "It spawned dozens of classic westerns, comedies and thrillers. Plus, it was the birthplace of film noir."

"Watch out, Bill," Jimmie teased, "your cinematic-nerd side's showing." He glanced at his flashy gold watch. "Gotta split. Told Bev I'd take her to the festival, play some of those games. She's hot about trying to win some grand prize cabin."

"Beach bungalow," corrected Ellie.

Jimmie nodded. "Yeah, that's right. I guess the winner gets a free rental there for the next two years."

"Ten," she corrected again. She hadn't realized she'd been so into it until this moment. Sure, she'd been willing to be Team Java Mammas with the girls, but she hadn't been *personally* driven to win anything other than the audition until this moment. Had to be the thought of hanging out with Bill for the rest of the afternoon, doing fun, wild things in some of those hot games.

And, if all went well, even more wild things afterward.

What Happens in Malibu Stays in Malibu.

"Ten, eh?" Jimmie gave a low whistle. "Now I'm glad I gave in and said yes to Bev." He snagged a cookie off the food table. "What time does the shoot start tomorrow?" he asked Bill.

"Five a.m. sharp. We need the rising sun in the background for that first shot."

Jimmie groaned. "Whoever said showbiz is glamorous needs their head checked." He pointed at his pal. "Watch out for that guy," he said to Ellie as he headed toward the tent opening.

Wouldn't Bill be surprised to know she'd been watching out for him for a long, long time.

After Jimmie left, Bill stared at Ellie, trying not to think how drop-dead sexy that fishnet cover-thing was over that red bikini. Very teasing. Very exciting.

Both of which were Ellie right now. All grown-up and hot and retro sexy in that peekaboo red bikini and matching shoes. Enough to make a man howl at the moon.

"What're you thinking about?" she asked.

With another woman, he might have said. But with Ellie…well, it was different. He wasn't exactly sure why, just knew he felt more protective. Of her, certainly. But also of their past. As though that bubble of time so long ago was more fragile than he'd realized.

"Hungry?" he asked.

"Famished."

"Me, too." He guided her toward the tent opening, his arm comfortably around her shoulders, their steps in sync. "Let's go to the festival and get some chow."

Ellie felt as though they'd walked this way a hundred times. His arm rested so easily around her, the side of his body seemed to fit perfectly against her. Muscles against curves, hard into soft.

When he leaned his head down, she caught a whiff of his cologne—cinnamon and musk—and nearly swooned at the rich, dark scent. Someone had once told her cinnamon was an aphrodisiac, and if she didn't believe it before, she sure did now.

"Something about you, Ellie," he murmured, his breath hot against her cheek.

She waited, but he didn't finish the thought. Even if he had, she doubted she'd have been able to stay focused and hear the words because she was caught up in sensations. His breath caressing her cheek, his thigh rubbing seductively against hers as they walked, that cinnamon scent shooting straight to the pleasure center of her brain.

They headed out into the blinding sunshine. The sand sank underneath her feet and she stumbled slightly.

"It's those sinister shoes," teased Bill, helping her regain her balance.

"I wasn't sure what to wear at the beach," she murmured.

"Coulda fooled me." He gave her an appreciative once-over, which gave her no small thrill.

She plastered on her best beach-babe smile, although she felt like a total fake. Except for the shoes. And the fishnet. And the tattoos, of course.

And how she felt every time she was near him.
Those feelings were as deep and real as they'd been
when she was a girl.

They faced each other, the heat from the sun
pouring down on them. In the distance, waves thun-
dered against the shoreline. A couple of teenagers
walked past, carrying umbrellas, towels and a radio
that was blasting Sheryl Crow singing how she just
wanted to have some fun.

So did Ellie. She'd started out telling herself this
week was about chilling, then about winning points and
being on her favorite show. But now all that paled to
what she really wanted—to be with Bill and have fun.
The kind of no-regrets, go-for-it fun she never allowed
herself. Now was the perfect time to indulge herself.

And he was the perfect man to indulge herself with.

Everything would be great, too, as long as she
kept up the facade, never let on that she lived in that
depressing vampire world where he assumed goths
resided. From what she'd gleaned, this was his only
afternoon off, so she didn't have to keep that facade
up for long anyway. A few hours, hopefully more.
Not a daunting task.

Although the thought of saying goodbye again was.

"Something wrong?" he asked, concern filling
his eyes.

She glanced at the coffee stain. "It's probably set
by now. Too late to get it out."

"Now, now, Ellie, so pessimistic," he kidded,
lightly rubbing her back.

She could feel the heat from his hand through the open spaces in the fishnet, warm and liquid against the bareness of her back. His touch was light, confident, exciting.

"We have bigger things to worry about than a coffee stain." He took her hand and started walking toward the festival. "Like what should we order for lunch?"

It'd been seventeen years since her maddening childhood crush. Seventeen years of remembering and fantasizing about Bill, and now all those memories and dreams and girlish yearnings coalesced into this single afternoon. If she ever had the opportunity to live in the moment, this was it. To revel in each moment, each minute, each hour.

Even if what happened in Malibu stayed in Malibu, she'd have the memories of this afternoon for the rest of her life.

4

GOING TO THE FESTIVAL was one thing.

Getting inside was another.

Ellie stood on the beach, the afternoon sun hot on her skin, her sweaty hand in Bill's, staring down the imposing-looking man blocking the festival side entrance. His size put him in the sumo wrestler league, and that patch over his eye gave him a Captain Barbossa in *Pirates of the Caribbean* look. If that combo wasn't bad enough, the words "You Lookin' at Me?" emblazoned on his tank top indicated either he had a rampant paranoia streak, or she would any moment.

"Go on in," murmured Bill, giving her hand a tug.

Digging her wedgies into the sand, she rasped, "Yeah, right, I've always wanted to die in Malibu."

"C'mon, Ellie. Thought you were hungry."

She averted her gaze in case Captain Sumo thought she was lookin' at him. "Can't we go in the main entrance?"

His eyebrows pressed together. "What's wrong with this one?"

"Like you need to ask."

With a low, throaty chuckle, he leaned his face close to hers. "I refuse to believe," he murmured, "that anyone who wears a Queen of Evil tattoo is afraid of walking past one itty-bitty security guard."

"Itty-bitty?" She blinked. "You've obviously been out in the sun too long."

He squeezed her hand. "Trust me on this, Ellie."

When they reached the guard, Bill paused, nodded a greeting. "How's it going, Sam?"

"It's cool, Bill."

"Mind if we go in?"

"You're the man." Sam stepped aside, motioned for them to enter.

They stepped inside a small tented area, the air cooled with the help of several rotating fans. Ellie stopped, brushed a strand of damp hair off her forehead. "So you two know each other."

"He's one of the security guys on the *Sin on the Beach* set."

"And you couldn't have shared that while I was freaking out?"

A rakish grin spread across his face. "Maybe I wanted to look big and bad in your eyes."

"Aren't you the macho one," she said with dry sarcasm.

"And you love it."

God help her, she did, even if she didn't want to give him the satisfaction of admitting it. She looked around the area, set up with folding chairs, coolers packed with ice and drinks, tables on which sat several monitors projecting black-and-white images of the festival. A buffed guy in shorts and a tank top with the word Security on its back sat viewing one of the monitors. He nodded hello to Bill, went back to his work.

"I feel like I'm with the in crowd," Ellie said, watching a group of people playing volleyball on one of the monitors. Maybe it was her imagination, but that brunette woman spiking the ball looked a lot like Candy.

"I know these guys from the *Sin on the Beach* set, where they work our security. I didn't know that was their special entrance, though." He looked over at the cooler. "Want a soda?"

"Should we—" But he was already heading over. Just like Bill to do what he wanted, screw the rules.

Watching him walk away made *her* forget any rules, too, as she admired the view. Broad, muscled back that narrowed to a fit waist. Great buns that shifted and moved under those khaki shorts. He had a bit of a bowlegged walk, like a cowboy, which made her smile. Unlike a cowboy, his legs were bare so she could see how compact and muscled they were.

She imagined gliding her palms down that muscled back, over that hard behind, around to his front where she'd dawdle…tease…explore….

He turned and she jerked her gaze up to his.

A slow, knowing grin danced across his face.

Caught. Well, so what? He'd probably seen plenty of women doing the same thing.

"Here you go," he said a moment later as he handed her a cold can of pop. "And dig this. Meat loaf sandwiches. I helped us to one." He handed a half to her. "Have a seat, relax." He leaned against a table and started munching.

She looked over her shoulder. "Should we—"

He motioned for her to sit, giving her a knowing nod as he ate.

She did, realizing she was doing that good-girl, what-are-the-rules thing again, which would never go over with a guy like Bill, who claimed his territory on the fly. Reminded her of the boys back in the hood and their power plays over turf—be it a porch, a street corner, a park. She wondered if Bill realized how, despite his so-called new life, he was still a boy in the hood.

For the next few minutes, they ate and drank in silence.

"This is delicious," she said, finishing a bite.

"You make meat loaf?"

She rolled her eyes. "Too busy. The only thing I make is coffee. You?"

"I make the best sandwiches this side of New York."

"Humble, aren't you?"

He grinned. "I prefer to call it truthful."

The guy watching the monitors had flipped on a portable radio to an oldies but goodies station. The upbeat, sexy song, "Walk on the Wild Side," started

playing. Same tune she'd downloaded for her ringtone. Perfect background music for sneaking glances
at Bill's mouth as he nibbled and chewed, at his
tongue as it flicked against his drink. She had no
doubt he could do incredible things with that mouth
in bed, too....

He lowered his soda. "Who's singing this song?"

"Lou Reed."

"That glam rock, punk guy?"

She heard the disdain in his voice, which put her
off a bit. Not that Bill should like the things she
liked, it was that he sounded so judgmental.

"That's old news," she said, not meaning to say it
so sharply, or maybe she did. "These days, he's respected for his songwriting, electronic music, even
his style of rock and roll."

He tapped his finger against the side of his drink.
"I offended you."

"Yes." She shrugged. "You sounded critical."

He stuffed the last bite of his sandwich into his
mouth. After finishing, he said, "You're honest. I
like that. I'm honest, too, sometimes to a fault, but I
like to be a man of my word, you know?"

Great. He revered honesty, and before him sat a
woman whose very appearance was a lie. She took
a sip of her drink, avoiding his eyes.

"I'm also a music dunce," he continued. "I'll
listen to tunes when I want to quiet my mind or relax,
but—" he shook his head "—it irritates me otherwise. Probably because I heard rap day and night

back in the hood. It was like crackling static that never went away. Songs about violence and sex and killing cops. I hated it. Ruined my appreciation for other kinds of music, I guess."

She remembered hearing rap when she was outside, but her world inside her bedroom was a sanctuary of what she liked—be it books or listening to Lou Reed or painting lyrics on her ceiling to her mother's annoyance. "Shame that happened. Music has often been my greatest solace."

"Lucky you."

For a moment they stared at each other, the sounds of the festival receding into the background, leaving the two of them suspended in a time capsule that encompassed the past and the present. She still saw the boy she'd been so crazy about, dark and handsome with a head full of dreams. But she also saw the man he'd become. Tougher, more cynical. A man who'd lost an appreciation of something as sweet and healing as music because he couldn't get past the grating static of his past.

She'd never imagined being with him again wouldn't be perfect. Of course, she was pitting her girlhood fantasies—which were always perfect—against the woman's newfound reality. And what she was learning was that for all the glowing feelings she experienced around Bill, there were also the darker ones.

Were they so dark she didn't want to stay? Because it'd be easy to make a lame excuse, walk away, dust her hands of the childhood fantasy.

She watched as he picked up their trash and tossed it in a receptacle, called out a thanks to Sam, patted the back of the guy who was still watching the monitors. Funny. For all his toughness, he was a caretaker. Just like her.

"Ready?" he said.

"For what?"

"For whatever's out there, of course." He gestured toward the tent opening that led to the festival.

Whoever said life had no guarantees should have added it would always have its fair share of confusion, too. Sometimes all that mattered was making a choice and hoping you made the right one. Okay, so he wasn't the boy of her childhood dreams; she wasn't the girl who'd dreamed them, either.

She took his hand, ready for whatever happened next.

A FEW MOMENTS LATER, they were walking down the midway. It was midafternoon, but the sun was still broiling as though it were high noon. Girls in bikinis and guys in shorts roamed the midway. Coconut-scented suntan lotion competed with the tangy salt air. Barkers and carnies pitched rides and games against a background of calliopes.

Bill interlaced his fingers with hers as he steered her through the crowd. Maybe because she typically dated more artistic types, or because she was accustomed to running her own business, she wasn't used to a guy taking the lead. She had to admit, though, that she liked his take-control attitude as he wove through the crowd, sometimes sheltering her past groups of partiers, other times hugging her close for no apparent reason.

Like she needed one.

"Hey you! Ms. Smoke and Fire! Black fishnet over the red bikini!"

"Is somebody talking to me?" asked Ellie, slowing down.

"That's right, I'm talking to you and that guy with the gravy stain on his shirt."

Bill laughed. "Talking to both of us, it appears."

They looked over at a small stage, on which stood the fellow in lime-green turban and loud Hawaiian shirt she'd seen earlier backstage at the audition.

"Yes, I'm talking to you." He eagerly waved them over. "Step this way."

Bill looked at Ellie. "You game?"

She looked at the sign over the stage. Magellan the All-Knowing. Although she'd always wanted to have a real supernatural experience, she'd never envisioned that might happen with a loudmouthed carnie at a beach festival.

"I don't know," she murmured.

"Maybe we'll win something."

"Don't be afraid," the man, who had to be Magellan, called out. "All that stands between fear and outcome is courage, my friends, courage!" He looked at the audience. "Right?"

The crowd started whistling and yelling.

"Courage, dudes, courage!"

"Don't be afraid!"

"Show your game!"

"We could have a mob scene if we don't do this," muttered Bill, taking Ellie's hand. "You down for this?"

"No tricks, nothing up my sleeve," continued Magellan, lifting the short sleeve of his shirt. He gestured to his turban. "Just the insights of my mind into your lives, and the mysteries I will foretell."

She squeezed Bill's hand. "What the hell? Let's go."

As they approached, people started whistling, slapping high-fives into the air. One guy, who looked as though he'd spent the better part of the day imbibing, gave a loud whoop.

"Wonderful, wonderful!" called out Magellan, welcoming them with open arms. "Come up here and stand next to me so I can read your vibes. Everyone, give these brave people a hand."

As the audience applauded, Magellan fumbled with the clip on the microphone, finally releasing it from his shirt. He held it toward Ellie. "Your name?"

"Ellie."

"Here on vacation?" This close, she noticed his handlebar mustache jiggled as he spoke.

"Yes."

"Funny, that's exactly what I was going to say!" People laughed. "Here with your husband?"

She felt heat crawl up her neck. "No."

Magellan gave the crowd a sly look. "Don't worry, your secret's safe with us." He looked back at Ellie, stared intently into her eyes. "With friends?"

"Yes."

"One of them is sweet like candy on—" he closed his eyes, then reopened them "—your cousin?"

Not cousin, her brother...but close enough to make her wonder if this guy might be the real thing. Maybe he really could tap into another dimension, understand secrets hidden from the ordinary eye....

Or Candy had already been up here today and blabbed about Ellie or Matt.

So much for other dimensions and hidden secrets.

"Something like that," Ellie said.

Magellan turned to Bill. "Your name?"

"Bill."

"Exactly what I was going to say!" The crowd laughed again, obviously enjoying the pretense of Magellan knowing all.

"So, tell us, Ellie and Bill, are you enjoying the festival?"

"Yes."

He stepped closer and peered into her face, as though reading her. Feeling a tad uncomfortable, she averted her gaze to his hands and a sparkling blue ring on his pinkie. Sapphire, she guessed.

"Yes," he whispered, "it's the stone of destiny."

Had he heard her thoughts?

She looked up, but Magellan was busy talking to the audience again, the blue stone sparkling with his gestures. He'd probably seen her looking at it, passed on the tidbit that it was the stone of destiny. Hardly a supernatural experience.

"So, Bill," Magellan said, "are you ready to play our game?"

"Depends."

"Ah!" Magellan made a swirling motion with his fingers again, reminiscent of an actor in a melodrama. "You're not one to believe in life's mysteries, and yet, deep down, you're curious if what is mystical and unseen might in fact be real."

"Not really."

The crowd laughed again.

"We'll see about that," said Magellan, taking a few steps away in his flip-flops. The guy was a mix of Jimmy Buffett and the Wizard of Oz. Too much.

"Time to play Truth or…Bare!" he announced to the crowd. "Which is a variation of Truth or Dare in honor of this very sexy *Sin on the Beach* festival."

Bill squeezed Ellie's hand. "Fasten your seat belt," he murmured, "'cause we're on the ride now."

"Ready?" Magellan asked them.

"Ready," they answered in unison.

"Wonderful." He closed his eyes, although she swore he was peeking out of one of them, and raised a forefinger to his turban as though summoning his powers. "I'm now calling on my spirit guides to reveal a secret about each of you. If I'm wrong—I mean, if my guides have erred—"

The crowd laughed.

"As I was saying, if my guides have erred, you earn fifty festival points as well as free tickets for rides." He reached into the air and—presto!—a string of tickets appeared.

Gasps from the crowd.

"However, if my spirit guides are right, which they usually are—" he looked over at Ellie and Bill "—that person must remove an item of clothing. Not a necklace, earring, ring, hat, belt, shoestring, sock or contact lens, but something major. We're talking the *bare* part of Truth or Bare, my brave friends."

Whoops and clapping.

She glanced at Bill, imagining what she'd like him to take off, first. Considering they were in public, his shirt would do.

But if they were alone…

"Ahem," Magellan said loudly into his microphone.

She looked over at him.

"The spirit guides say 'naughty, naughty'!"

Even she had to laugh. Psychic insight? Nah. He'd caught her checking out Bill, every wanton little thought written all over her face.

Magellan turned dramatically solemn. "It's time for the spirits to speak."

As he put his palms together at his heart level, a flutter of flutes and harps swelled. She figured he'd touched some wireless remote hidden in his breast pocket that triggered the music. She wondered what other buttons he had hidden on his body, and what those might do.

Magellan nodded as though listening to someone speaking. Finally, he opened his eyes and put a hand on each of their shoulders. The music rose, the notes twirling higher and higher…

Then abruptly stopped.

"They've spoken," Magellan said dramatically. "To you, Bill."

A woman in the crowd shrieked.

"She's not my spirit guide, by the way," Magellan said under his breath, the aside accidentally on purpose muttered directly into the microphone. The crowd ate it up, laughing and clapping.

"The spirits have a riddle for you, Bill. Listen carefully. What has roots nobody sees, is taller than trees, its virtues it sows and yet never grows?"

Bill's eyebrows shot up in surprise. "They said all that?"

Magellan shrugged. "They're a little wordy sometimes. They say when you find the answer, you'll also find your destiny. But so you can play Truth or Bare, they also told me a secret. Yes or no. Your friend, they say, based a character in a story on you?"

Bill blinked, nodded. "That's right. No way you could have checked that on the Internet. Awesome trick, man."

"No trick, my friend. I'm merely a vessel for the spirit guides. So, what item of clothing will it be, Bill?"

He tapped the stain on his shirt. "I've been meaning to take this off ever since I spilled coffee on it this morning, so…" He grabbed the end of the polo shirt and tugged it over his head.

A thrill zigzagged through Ellie as she stared at his chest. His muscled, brown and deliciously hairy chest.

But it was the tattoo that made her blood run molten.

The dragon's mighty torso, a marvel of blues and greens, crested over Bill's shoulder, its reptilian head lying seductively across the pec, flames of fire shooting across his breastbone.

Women in the audience went nuts. Ellie hadn't heard that much screaming since her girlfriend's bachelorette party, the night she lost fifty dollars tipping a male stripper named Robby Rawhide.

"Your turn," said Magellan, facing her.

With some difficulty, she tore her gaze off Bill. "Shoot," she rasped.

"The spirits say your age is twenty-nine."

Pause. "That's it? A number?"

Magellan nodded.

She felt slighted. Bill got the riddle, then the insight about being the model for a character. And the spirits only guessed her age?

Which was correct, but too easy. Oh, yeah, definitely the work of Candy, the marketing whiz. She'd probably left a few tidbits about Ellie and Sara with Magellan to boost Team Java Mamma's chance of winning. Maybe someone on *Sin on the Beach* had done something similar—left a cheat sheet with Magellan, giving names, descriptions, a few planted facts about people who worked on the show. It made Magellan look good, boosted attendance at his performances, which in turn raked in money for *Sin on the Beach.* A win-win all the way around.

Darn. She'd so hoped for something really supernatural, but it appeared Magellan was just a carnie with connections.

"Yes, I'm twenty-nine."

Applause.

Magellan made a grand flourish. "Choose a piece of clothing."

A no-brainer. Her fishnet cover-up. She slipped it off to much clapping and whistles. She caught Bill's approving look, which pleased her.

She glanced at his shorts, he glanced at her top. Those would be the next pieces to go. An idea she liked. A lot. Just not *here.*

"I'm getting another message from the guides," announced Magellan.

"Uh," said Ellie, not wanting to hang here any longer, "tell them thanks but no thanks?"

Bill chuckled. "C'mon, Ellie. We don't want to hurt their feelings."

Magellan, his forefinger pressed against his turban like some kind of divining rod, closed his eyes. "They're speaking…. Okay, here's the message. Cinderella doesn't make it home before midnight, but that's not the end of her story."

The hairs tingled on the back of her neck. She'd thought of Cinderella and her prince an hour or so ago…one of those funny thoughts that flits in and out of one's head…but how odd to hear Magellan reference Cinderella, too.

"Is that my riddle?" she asked quietly.

Magellan gave her such a focused look, she swore he could read every thought she'd ever had.

"No," he finally said, "it's more of an insight. But because it wasn't a question that can be answered, you win the prize and the points." A festival ride ticket materialized in his hand, which he handed to Ellie along with a voucher for points.

As they walked back into the crowd, Bill hugged her close against his side. "Way to go, Ellie. You've won points at the audition, and now Truth or Bare!"

"Yeah, it's great." But she didn't feel as exuberant as she sounded because now she had Cinderella on the brain. Everybody knew it wasn't until the very end of the story that Cinderella didn't make it home by midnight….

Didn't the story pretty much end there?

5

SEVERAL HOURS LATER, Ellie and Bill had ridden the merry-go-round, gotten dizzy on the Tilt-A-Whirl, slipped and laughed down the gigantic blow-up slide. They'd watched people play volleyball, bowl with coconuts and jiggle and bounce on a community-size trampoline. Ellie had tried her luck at the ring toss and Bill had tested his strength swinging the mallet at the Hi-Striker.

After all that, they were content to simply walk hand in hand down the midway, sipping their lemonades. Bill wore his shirt tied around his waist, Ellie's fishnet cover-up draped over his shoulder, items of clothing they hadn't put back on since Truth or Bare.

He stopped and looked at her. "You'll probably think this sounds crazy, because I see bodies in bikinis all day long." He pulled her cover-up off his shoulder and held it up. "But seeing yours through a sexy fishnet…" He blew out a pent-up breath. "Well, it makes it extra sexy."

"Hold my drink," she said, handing hers to him.

The speed with which she took the fishnet out of his hands made him laugh.

"You want it," she said with a smile, "you got it." She slithered into it, wriggling this way and that, which only added to the heat he'd been feeling ever since she strolled onto the stage this morning.

Those big turquoise eyes glistened as she looked at him, and suddenly he recalled those same big eyes from many years ago as a much younger Ellie asked if it was true...was he really moving away to New York?

He remembered how he'd felt that summer when he was eighteen, so damn anxious to move away and be on his own, it was all he could do to stay put. Once he'd landed in New York, he'd sworn never to go back. And he'd kept his word. His mom and sisters had occasionally visited him, but he'd never returned. In fact, until today, he'd rarely thought of the hood.

Yet spending time with Ellie had brought back memories—too many memories—of where they'd grown up. It brought back the memories of gunshots and kids dealing drugs and rap music and...

Then there was the resurrected memory of a young girl who'd lived next door, all gangly and wide-eyed and interested in the fate of a boy she barely knew.

That girl had been sweet, but the rest of the memories were sour. Getting closer to her didn't mean getting closer to the rest of his past. Or did it?

"What is it?" Ellie asked.

He played with the fishnet, slipping his fingers

through the diamond-shaped knit, feeling as tangled up in his emotions as he did in the threads. He dug her, was more drawn to and excited by her than he'd been to a woman in a long time, and yet…

She frowned slightly as she studied his face. "Are you feeling ill?"

He almost laughed, more at his own mishmash of thoughts than her question. He looked around at the crowd of people, some laughing, some eating, others kissing….

"This isn't the place," he said quietly.

"For what?"

He knew what he was about to say would come out sounding harsh, but he didn't have a choice. Better to say it now, before things went further.

"This afternoon's been great, but…"

"But…"

"I can't do this."

"This meaning…*me?*"

He nodded. Emotion filled her eyes and he went from feeling like a jerk to feeling like a rat.

"You can't spend any more time with me," she clarified, keeping her voice level.

He released a slow breath. "Right."

Her chin quivered, but just when he thought she might crumble, she gave him such a long, judicious look, he realized he was dealing with a woman who might look soft, but could be tough-minded when necessary.

"I was confused about you, too," she said simply.

In the distance, wheezy calliope music and the clang, clang, clang of a bell scraped against his nerves.

"Want to share why?" he finally asked, hearing his defensiveness and telling himself it wasn't because his male ego had just been dinged.

"You first."

He puffed out a breath. "Great, put me on the spot."

"You started it."

"I did." He belatedly realized his fingers were still enmeshed in her fishnet cover-up. He looked down the peekaboo crisscross pattern, past it at her plump breasts, the taut tummy, those nicely shaped legs. "Oh, yes, I did start this, didn't I...."

He dragged his gaze back to hers. In a low, rough voice, he murmured, "It's not that you're not so hot I couldn't lay you right here."

Her eyes widened, the pupils dark. "Wow," she murmured, "you'd like to do me right here and now, but you can't spend any more time with me."

"I'm not *that* callous, Ellie."

"No, just full of yourself."

He looked behind them at a bench next to a taco truck. "Look, this conversation is weird enough without us standing in the midway surrounded by dozens of beach partygoers. Want to sit down?"

"Sure."

A few moments later, they sat next to each other on the bench. Scents of fried onions and spices saturated the air. Across the way, people were lining up for a limbo contest.

"It's been such a nice day," Ellie finally said, "how about we bypass the heavy conversation, agree we can't do this, and enjoy the next few minutes."

He suddenly felt hollow. "All right," he said quietly.

She gestured at the noisy, crowded midway. "Reminds me of that old movie *Carnival Story*."

"Anne Baxter, nineteen-fifty-four. Not too many people remember that film."

He'd never dated a woman who liked the Golden Age of Hollywood, not with any depth anyway. Most actresses equated those years with Marilyn Monroe, not with films or lesser-known actors of substance.

"Look at that guy." Ellie pointed at a middle-aged, round-faced man walking down the midway with a tray loaded with baked items. "Reminds me of the bakers who'd bring their pastries to the festivals on Olvera Street, near where we lived. Oh, I can almost taste them now—what were they called?"

In East L.A., Olvera, with its cobblestone, pedestrian-only street, was famous for its multicultural festivals and celebrations, from Cinco de Mayo to Christmas to the Chinese New Year.

"Pan dulce," he said, the memory of the Mexican sweet breads making his mouth water. "Remember how they'd stick to the roof of your mouth?

"Yes. Remember the Christmas Eve procession?" asked Ellie. "Afterward, there'd be several hundred kids breaking piñatas and scrambling for candy."

He nodded, remembering his siblings laughing

and grabbing candy while he, big brother and man of the house, watched over them. He didn't want to be lured into the memories, didn't want to look back, but that was like not wanting to swim with the tide. The pull was too strong.

"I especially liked the Ferris wheel. Even though I got kicked off it more than I got to actually ride it." He shook his head, remembering some of the dumb stunts he pulled. "It's been years since I've been on one."

"Sometimes people would wear costumes, too."

"A lot of those people just *looked* like they were wearing costumes." He made a disapproving noise. "Some of the girls wore so much makeup and tats, they looked like they should be in the band KISS!" He laughed.

"My favorite celebration," said Ellie, "was the Dia de Los Muertos. That's how it's pronounced, right?"

"You said it just like a homie, *chiquita*." Dia de Los Muertos. Day of the Dead. The Mexican celebration to honor those no longer living.

For a moment, the crush of people and sounds and scents were almost like the festivals of years ago... almost. Some people in his past were no longer living, and even though he thought of them, he'd done little to honor them. An old shame bubbled up that he'd tried to bury so many times.

"So," Ellie said, "what is it you wanted to talk about?"

"Bill!" squealed a female voice.

Phoebe, aka Diane, wiggled up to them wearing a white bikini that was barely legal.

"Fiona," said Bill.

Her smiled drooped. "Phoebe."

"Right," he muttered, scratching a spot on his chin.

Ellie wished she and Bill were standing because from their seated perspective, they had a ringside seat to Phoebe's bodacious mounds that threatened to spill right out of her top.

Phoebe glanced at Ellie, back to Bill. "Having another meeting?"

"No."

"Good," she said, batting her eyes. "Because I have a problem and was hoping you could help me."

Ellie couldn't believe her eyes. She thought this kind of big-man-can-you-save-me act only happened in the movies. Really bad, cheesy movies.

Bill shifted, cleared his throat. "Uh, what's the problem?"

To Ellie's shock and wonder, Phoebe-Diane leaned over just enough to give Bill a dead-on cleavage shot.

He glanced down, back up to Phoebe's face. And said...nothing.

Ellie had to remind herself that men were made of flesh and blood. Offer a man a boob-flash and he'd look. Shame Phoebe wasn't a rap song.

"I was supposed to enter the Hot Shot Photo Scavenger Hunt with a friend," Phoebe said in a baby-talk singsong voice, "but he couldn't make it." She put on a sad look, which consisted of sticking out her bottom lip and making a noise like a pigeon cooing.

Unbelievable. No goth chick in her right mind would pull that stunt.

"Everyone's signing up for the Hot Shot Photo Scavenger Hunt in an hour," continued Phoebe, as though someone had asked for details. "That's when they give everyone the text number where to send their photos. One category is tattoos, another tan lines—" she ran her finger along the edge of her bikini top "—stuff like that. And the photos are flashed on the screens." She leveled a look at Bill. "Want to be my partner?"

Ellie took a big sip of her lemonade, making a loud slurping noise. When Bill looked at her, she gave a couldn't-help-it shrug.

"Sorry, Phoebe," he said, turning back to her. "But I made other plans."

"Later, then?"

"Look," Bill said, gesturing to the crowds of people, "there's at least two guys for every woman here. Just hold up a sign, and you'll have a partner within seconds."

"But…" She pouted. "I wanted *you* to be my partner."

Bill took Ellie's hand. "I already have one."

Ellie's very breath scattered and for a moment she couldn't breathe, couldn't move, couldn't think. Well, not for long. A coherent thought finally took shape in her mind. *Wasn't this the confused guy who'd decided he couldn't do this with me?*

Yeah, and she was the confused girl who hadn't been too sure about giving this a chance, either.

She interlaced her fingers with his and smiled to herself. Maybe two wrongs didn't make a right, but two confused people could certainly make a go of it.

A SHORT WHILE LATER, Ellie and Bill stood in front of a ticket booth. The sun was hovering low in the early evening sky. Neon lights were coming to life along the midway.

Ellie looked up at the Ferris wheel then back to Bill. "Think you can behave so we don't get kicked off?"

"I'll do my best." He grinned. "Can't make any promises, though."

"Candy and Sara are expecting us at the Hot Shot game in thirty minutes, so let's try not to be escorted out of the festival, okay?"

"Hey, look on the bright side. If we get kicked off, who will be escorting us out of the festival? Our pals at Security." He winked. "So all we need to do is put on a good show, pretend we're really leaving, then turn around and sneak back in."

She gave him a teasing look. "And you claim to be such an honest man."

"Ellie," he said, lifting her hand, "I'm always honest when it comes to you." He placed a kiss on the back of her fingers.

She closed her eyes and shuddered a release of

breath, liking the feel of his lips against her skin even as she didn't like her own deceit. *Wait a minute—how bad am I really being? Lots of women, and men, dress or act a certain way to attract the opposite sex.*

The justification, however, felt hollow. In a way, she felt more manipulative than Phoebe, whose dress and behavior were an extension of herself, whereas Ellie was being something she wasn't.

"You okay?"

"Huh? Oh, sure." Not.

"We don't have to go on the Ferris wheel."

"No, I want to." *The longer we're together, the greater the chances he'll figure out my deceit.*

Neither moved. He gave her a quizzical look. "Something's wrong, I can tell. Do you want to talk about it?"

"Stop," she said softly, pressing her finger to his lips.

He liked the soft feel of her touch against his mouth. He imagined nibbling a little on her finger, slowly sucking it into his mouth, running his tongue around it.

He grew hard again just thinking about where else she could put her hands…where else he could put his mouth.

She must have picked up on his thoughts because she slowly ran her finger along his top lip, trailing along the cushion of his bottom lip, down to his soul patch.

"I like this," she said, lightly feathering the patch.

"I like you touching it."

Her fingers trailed to his jaw. "The reason I'm acting oddly is…this will be over soon."

"Who said?"

"Me." She dropped her hand. "Our crossing paths in Malibu was total serendipity."

"So?"

She took a breath. "So, considering how busy we are the rest of this week—well, you more than me—it's sheer luck we have the rest of today to spend together. I mean, sure, we'll probably see each other on the set, but from a distance. Then the week will end, we'll return to our routines, and that's that."

He raised his eyebrows. "Gee, Ellie, your romantic streak is showing."

She laughed softly. "I'm being realistic. Like Cinderella at the ball, midnight will strike and it will all be over."

"So, this ends at midnight?"

She shrugged, nodded.

"But I thought Magellan said Cinderella doesn't make it home before midnight."

"Yeah, but Magellan is nothing more than a Jimmy Buffett character in a turban."

One could never say Ellie was an easy-to-read woman, which appealed to Bill even if it had its frustrating moments. He'd always liked a challenge, and Ellie certainly gave him that.

Amazing, she was offering him a tidy ending. No strings. What he would have given for other women to have offered him the same deal. Problem was, with Ellie, he wanted more. He never thought he'd admit this to himself, but he'd enjoyed their reminiscences about Olvera Street, down to how the *pan dulce* stuck to the roofs of their mouths.

What other memories would they share? Friends they'd known? Family they'd loved…and those they'd lost? No, she was right. It was better to put a lid on this before it got out of hand.

"Okay," he said, "we go with your plan. At the stroke of midnight, that's it."

She nodded, a look of relief in her eyes.

Which irked him. She didn't have to look *relieved* about it. Unless…there was something he was missing in this picture.

"Have to ask…is there a boyfriend? Don't mind making a deal, as long as it's a fair deal and we're both putting our cards, so to speak, on the table."

"No, I'm not involved with anyone. Man or woman, just to set the record straight." She smiled teasingly, then turned somewhat serious. "How about you?"

"Same. Except, well, to be honest…" He scratched his chin. "There's someone I recently dated, but it's in limbo."

She narrowed her eyes. "Define limbo."

"She, uh, wants to see if there's potential, but I'm not so sure."

"Potential? As in, meet the mother?"

He'd never taken anyone to meet his mother. "Something like that."

She mulled it over for a moment. "Okay, we stick with the midnight plan. But no sex."

"What?"

She gave him an incredulous look. "You're the one leading on Ms. Limbo."

"No, no, you're misconstruing the entire thing. Limbo means nothing's happening." He blew out a breath. "I can't believe we're having yet another weird conversation in the middle of the midway."

"But you're involved," she said, ignoring his aside.

"We *were* dating. Past tense."

She arched a brow. "Does she know you speak of her in the past tense?"

"What does it matter? We're over at midnight, anyway!" He started to scratch his chin, paused, dropped his hand. Too late. Laser-eyes had tracked the move.

"Look," he said, "as dumb as this conversation is, I'm a man of my word and I'm giving it to you here, now, straight up. Vi and I met, we dated for a few months. We both have demanding careers, the commute to each other's place is a hassle, so we're taking a break while she's in Europe. When she gets back, we're going to see where things are."

Ellie felt her world topple a little. "Vi?"

"Short for Violette."

The way he said it, made the name sound…

"She's French?"

Bill nodded.

"Accent and all that?"

"Yes, accent and—" he gave a shake of his head, a slight smile curving his lips "—all that, whatever that's supposed to mean."

It means that she's tall, lithe, makes a mouth-watering coq au vin that makes men fall to their knees, and she knows more sexual tricks than the Kama Sutra.

Rubbing her eyebrow, Ellie looked around, not wanting Bill to see the disappointment in her face. Disappointment, ha, to see the flat-out, Oz-green jealousy. She needed a moment to tame her inner beasts, rein them before they got the better of her.

Okay, there's another woman waiting in the wings. Bottom line, do you believe the limbo part?

She thought about his eyes when he'd said it. They glistened with such earnestness. A memory flashed in her mind. A sixteen-year-old Bill, going around the neighborhood looking for his kid sister.

Ellie had stood behind her mom and watched him as he paced on the porch, worried, talking about his sister, her bad report card, how she'd run away from home. He hadn't been as tall or buffed as now, but already handsome in that dark, intense way.

That day, he'd also had the same look in his eyes as he had now.

Yeah, she believed him about Vi.

"Ellie?"

She turned, met his gaze. "Okay, midnight plan is still on."

"With…or without?"

She gave a slow, teasing grin. "Bill Romero, do you think I waited this long to go without?"

6

BILL'S TEETH FLASHED white against his bronze skin. "Cool!" He grabbed Ellie into a hug, laughing. "We'll boogie down until the midnight hour, baby!"

His exuberance was infectious. Ellie laughed with him, any lingering reservations dissolving into the warm evening air. "Boogie down and up and every which other way!"

A sunburned guy in a loud Hawaiian shirt, white sunblock on his nose, stopped, his mouth agape. "Wow, dudes, what contest is that?"

Ellie and Bill turned and looked at him.

"Man, I'd like to sign up for that midnight boogie game." He took a sip from a bright red straw stuck into a coconut. "Where's it at?"

"Keep heading in the direction you're going." Ellie pointed in case he wasn't sure. "When you pass the volleyball games, take a left."

"Cool!" He teetered, caught his balance. "What's the contest name?"

Ellie and Bill looked at each other.

Bill turned back to the guy. "Twelve strokes to midnight."

Ellie, taking a sip of her lemonade, nearly choked.

"Righteous." The guy flashed them a hang ten before disappearing into the crowd.

Ellie gave Bill a look. "Twelve strokes to midnight?"

He grinned, obviously enjoying his impromptu quip. "It would have made a perfect contest name for this festival." He suddenly grew serious. "Hey, sorry about that funky mood I was in earlier."

"Like I don't have my funky moments, too."

"Yeah, you do," he teased. "I blame mine on my fiery, passionate Cuban half, what's your excuse?"

She laughed, pressed her cool lemonade container against his bare chest. He barely flinched, macho guy that he was.

"I don't have one unless I can blame it on my Irish half. The other half is very repressed, Midwestern."

"Yeah, I'd barely ever hear a peep from your house."

"How could you? The Romeros were the loudest family on the block!"

People were disembarking the Ferris wheel, couples looking flushed, their hair windblown. Some were laughing, others walking slowly with their arms wrapped around each other.

A man, dressed in denim shorts and a red-and-white striped tank top, strolled in front of the gate to the ride, calling out to the crowd. "Get your tickets to the Ferris wheel! A lucky few get a special stop at the top! Step right up, get your tickets!"

Bill dug into his pocket, pleased when he found the last few complimentary tickets. He held them up.

"C'mon, Ellie, let's go misbehave."

MINUTES LATER, a squat sixty-something man who managed to talk while chewing the butt of a cigar, admonished them not to stand up "till da ride stops" before shutting the metal bar over their laps with a heavy clang. The ride lurched, their benchlike seat jerked up several feet, then it stopped abruptly to load the next passengers.

"Don't stand up till da ride stops."

Clang.

Their seat lurched upward another few feet, stopped, swinging slightly.

Ellie, her fingers gripped around the cold metal bar, stared straight ahead, feeling slightly giddy. The ride lurched up again. Her stomach clenched.

"Nervous?" asked Bill, putting his arm around her.

"A little."

"Let's get your mind onto something else, then. Tell me about your coffee shop. What's the name of it?"

"Dark Gothic Roast."

"Gothic, huh? Why'd you pick that?"

Lurch. Her stomach rose with the chair until it jerked to another stop. They were high enough that she could see the ocean, a vast dark blue all the way to the horizon.

"Because..." She could tell him a little without giving away her secret. "...I like that era. The somber but emotional art, the great cathedrals, the stained glass."

"Sounds cool. Where is it?"

He could look it up online, or in the telephone book, so she might as well tell him. Anyway, she doubted he'd ever show up. It was in one of L.A.'s high-rise business areas—lots of tall buildings and people in suits. Anyway, unless her business loan fell through, she'd soon be moving it.

"Century City."

"So you cater to the eight-to-five types."

"Yes." The suits got a kick out of the goth theme. Some even held business meetings there. The bulk of her evening clientele came from the goth bar around the corner.

She held her breath as their bench seat rose, rose....

They stopped at the top.

"This is awesome." Cool breezes whipped her hair. Hot sun beat on her skin. She felt fantastic— more alive, more exhilarated than she had in a long time...years, actually.

He squeezed her shoulder, hugged her closer. She turned slightly and looked at him. Maybe it was the bright sun, but she felt as though she saw more in his face. A brooding restlessness, a loneliness, she hadn't noticed before. As though no place were home.

He smiled, the lines crinkling around his eyes, and the restlessness disappeared. "You okay?"

She nodded, still a bit taken aback at the glimpse she'd just seen.

"I can signal the guy to stop the ride when we're back down." His gaze dropped to her lips, slowly returned to her face.

"No," she murmured, "I'm fine."

She snuggled closer just as the ride started to descend. Wind rushed up to meet them as a thrill shimmied from her stomach all the way to the top of her head. She pressed against Bill and emitted a high, piercing shriek that she couldn't have held back if she'd tried.

Then, they swept past the ground, the blur of people and noises and smells fading away into the distance as they soared up, up, up to the blue sky and a yellow sun.

She wrapped her arms around Bill's waist, the feel of his warm skin grounding her in the dizzying rush of wind and light.

When he tightened his hold, she took advantage of it to snuggle closer. Her cheek slid down slightly, resting on his hard, molded pec. She looked into the tattooed dragon's eye, fierce and blue, the burnished green scales trailing behind. Such a big, bad dragon. She flicked out her tongue and licked it.

Salty. Warm.

Another thrill rushed through her as the ride soared skyward again. Higher, higher. She buried her head against his chest as another high-pitched shriek ripped loose from her lips.

As they crested, she felt more than heard his chuckle rumble up his chest.

"Hold on," he yelled, tightening his hold on her as they plummeted back to earth.

She didn't want to look. Didn't dare look. Instead, she hung on to Bill for dear life, clamping shut her mouth to stop further banshee screams.

Then, suddenly, they jerked to a stop.

As the bench seat swung back and forth for a moment, she kept her face buried against his chest.

"You all right?"

She raised her head. All she saw was Bill's face, creased with a wide grin.

"You're laughing at me."

"No." He tried not to grin, but his mouth refused. "Sorry, it's just...have you ever thought about doing voice-over work? Some actors actually specialize in screams."

"Very funny." She straightened a little and looked around. They were on the backside of the ride, which was a good thing because it helped center her somewhat to see all the other passengers in front and above them. "Why are we stopped?"

Bill looked down. "Nobody's getting on." He turned back to her.

When their eyes met, she was taken with how much lighter his brown eyes were than she remembered. Maybe because their faces were so close, or because of the bright light, but their color reminded her of the rich caramel she sometimes drizzled on coffee drinks.

Like caramel, the look in his eyes was sweet, too. Funny, he had more personalities than she did. The temperamental Cuban. The macho guy. And now, the sweet man with the tender, almost hopeful, look in his eyes.

Then, something odd happened as she realized that it wasn't that she was seeing something new, but that he'd let her get inside him. Not much, but enough to be vulnerable to her. Enough to trust her. Instinctively she knew he didn't give that away too often, if at all.

They sat that way for a long moment, their eyes silently probing, deeply, into the other's.

When another gust blew her hair into her eyes, he swept the strands back. But his hand remained, gently cupping her face.

"Ellie," he murmured, "you're so beautiful."

Beautiful had always seemed a word for other women, not her. Sometimes, in her goth attire and makeup, she fancied herself darkly exotic. But as a beach babe, she felt like a plastic Barbie doll.

But to hear it from Bill's lips, with that look in his eyes…she felt beautiful.

He lowered his head to kiss her and she eagerly raised her lips to meet his. And when they were so close she could almost taste him…

A cell phone rang.

Bill cursed under his breath. "With the shoot starting tomorrow, I need to be on call for any last-minute problems." Pulling back from their almost kiss, he rummaged in his shorts' pocket for the phone as it rang again. He frowned, looked up at Ellie.

"That's not my ringtone. It's some guy singing about taking a walk on the wild side."

"Oh! That's my Lou Reed ringtone." She'd been in such a fog with Bill, she hadn't recognized it. Didn't mean she wanted to answer it. But then, Candy or Sara might need her. She retrieved the phone from her purse. "Hello?"

"El, it's Tish. We've run out of Count Chocula cereal, I couldn't find any at the store, which means we're going to have a lot of pissed-off people in the morning."

She'd missed her long-dreamed-of kiss over Count Chocula? "You called me about that?"

Big sigh. "No, there's more. The moving guys dropped by, said they need a deposit to move Dark Gothic Roast to its new location. I told them it's not a done deal, but they said they need a deposit, which is refundable, to hold that time slot."

"Okay, fine, write a check."

"Where are they again?"

Tish, short for Morticia, was great with people, organized, but her memory was riddled with more holes than a body-piercing parlor.

"Office desk, third drawer down on the right."

"So, when's our big move again?"

"We'll probably be relocating in a month, tops. Just waiting for the loan approval."

"Groovy. How's it going?"

"Can't talk. I'm on a Ferris wheel."

"You? On a Ferris wheel?"

"Yeah, me. Bye." She hung up, not wanting to waste a single moment more of Bill, who was staring up at something.

"Figured out why we're stopped." He pointed upward. "It's one of the lucky couples who get extra time at the top."

Ellie looked. Over the edge of the seat at the very top, a bikini top dangled from someone's hand.

"What happens on the Ferris wheel," murmured Ellie, "stays on the Ferris wheel?"

Bill chuckled. "Not if she lets go of that top. Hey, what was that about relocating?"

"If my business loan goes through, I'll be moving the coffee business. I was waiting to hear before sharing the news with anyone. Even my brother doesn't know yet."

"To where?"

If she told him the complete truth, he'd lose it. So she fudged. "Inland."

The ride started up again. This time when Bill wrapped his arm around her, she cuddled next to him but didn't hide her eyes. Instead, every time they crested over the top of the ride, she drank in the awe-inspiring view of the coast and beach and endless ocean.

The fourth time around, as they started to crest, the ride slowed...and stopped.

She gasped, turned to Bill.

"Let's see if what happens in the Ferris wheel stays there," he murmured, wrapping his arms around her.

Up high, the blazing sun warmed her skin, but that paled compared to the heat exploding within her.

Bill smiled down at her and she responded, as best her trembling lips could. Foggily, she realized she was gripping his shoulders, as though if she didn't hold on for dear life she might float away.

He turned his head slightly, lowered it, angled his mouth to hers. She raised her mouth to his in silent compliance, moaning slightly at the pressure of his warm, firm lips. Tasting him, she leaned right into him, her body quivering with anticipation.

He didn't stop at a quick, chaste kiss, but eased her mouth open and slid his tongue inside. His tongue was smooth and nimble, flicking the corners of her mouth, sliding across her teeth, seeking and searching, an explorer claiming the new land.

Her tongue joined in, sinuously curling around, over, under his. The dance slow, inviting, gentle, its pleasurable sensations rippling through her until they pooled hot between her legs.

No big surprise. Bill Romero knew how to kiss.

Pulling back, he threaded his hand through her hair. "Like spun gold," he murmured.

For a moment she wasn't sure what he was talking about. Oh, right. The beach babe hair.

He lifted several strands and kissed them. "I feel like a miser with his fortune."

"Yeah, well, not everything that shines like gold is gold."

He blinked, let her hair slide from his fingers. "Ellie, you going heavy on me?"

She smiled. "That was my half-Irish side. It spouts heavy thoughts sometimes."

With an amused look, he cupped the side of her face, lifting her head slightly so she was looking directly at him, then let his hungry gaze travel slowly over her breasts, down her torso, settling in that region between her legs. Being up here alone, away from prying eyes, she felt aroused and bold. What happens in Malibu stays in Malibu.

She spread her legs slightly, a quiet dare. *Your move.*

He made a guttural sound that resonated down to her very nerve endings.

"Nice," he murmured. He lightly touched the fishnet stretched over where he was staring. "I have an idea."

Just imagining what he might be thinking made her go wet. "Yes?" Hardly a question. She was so hot, so worked up, she was game for anything.

He reached for her and she tensed in anticipation. "I'll take this," he said, slipping her cell phone from her hold.

"You want to *call* somebody at a time like this?"

He chuckled under his breath. "No, I want to take some photos for that Hot Shot game. My phone doesn't have a built-in camera, but I noticed yours does."

She wasn't sure whether to feel turned-on or pissed off. What happened to that great, warmer-up kiss? That boogie-till-midnight oath?

He peered at the phone. "I'd rather get down and

dirty, but it could get dangerous trying to pull our clothes back on while plummeting back to earth."

Much better. She pointed at the phone. "Press the button that says Camera, then point and shoot. Here, let me get a shot of your dragon." She took it, showed the image to Bill in the miniscreen, then handed it to him. "Your turn."

"Hmm…can you turn away just a little? Enough to get a shot of your Queen of Evil tattoo?"

She shifted, her breath catching at the expanse of sky and sea, a little afraid, a lot excited to be testing herself in more than one way. "How's that?"

"Perfect…I'll just slip your bikini bottom down a little…oh, yeah…"

She shivered as his warm fingers brushed against her tushy.

"Okay, turn back."

As she did, he rose slightly in his chair. She grabbed his leg. "Bill, you can't stand—"

"Till da ride stops, I know. I'm not standing, just hovering a little higher than usual."

"No wonder you got kicked off the ride," she whispered, not wanting to look down, see how far he could fall.

And yet, when she looked back at him…she was impressed. Not only with his gutsiness, but his obvious calling as a director. He had a way with the camera, moving just so until he framed the shot, a man with a vision that would not be denied.

Holding on to the back of their seat, he leaned

back against the bar. "Bend over a little…let me see that spiderweb tattoo through the fishnet."

She quickly did as told before her last sight of Bill Romero was him pitching into the sky.

He clicked as he talked. "Great… Lift your fishnet…fantastic…now, show me that wicked little spiderweb tattoo…good…can you take a deep breath?"

She leaned back slightly and inhaled deeply, causing the edge of the spiderweb to swell slightly over her red bikini top.

"Nice," he murmured. "A little more?"

She pulled the edge of her top down, just a little, exposing more of the tattoo.

"More," he said.

It was exciting being up here in their private little world, playing this sexy game. This was a new Ellie, not the one who put others first, but a woman putting herself first as she indulged her fantasies.

No judgments, no repercussions. Just free to enjoy and experiment and…

Be bold.

She pulled down the bikini top, showing more of the tattoo, more of her breast.

"That's good," murmured Bill, taking another photo.

She pulled it down farther.

Her nipple, hard and aroused, popped out. The impact of cool air tingled against her skin, the sensation hardening her nub.

Bill all but crashed back into his seat, his mouth

open. "Oh, yes, baby," he murmured, tracing his blunt nail around the pebbled areola, his sensual touch shooting heat straight to her groin. Holding down her top, she sucked in a shaky breath watching his dark hand against her exposed white flesh, watching his circling path tighten, draw closer to the nipple.

"Do you like that?"

"Yes," she shuddered.

He lightly flicked his finger over the nipple. She gasped with pleasure.

Suddenly, metal clanked. As the ride shuddered, began to move, she started to pull her top back up.

"Not so fast," growled Bill. He leaned down and took a gentle bite of the fullness, then trailed a sensuous path to the nipple, which he flicked, once, twice.

Wind rushed past, sounds from below sharpened.

"Bill," she murmured.

"Not yet…"

His big dark hand squeezed her breast, guided its pebbled nub into his wet, warm mouth. It felt forbidden to be doing this so exposed, in danger of being caught, which only excited her more as she watched him lap and suckle.

The sounds of the festival grew louder.

"Bill," she gasped.

He raised his head and smiled at her, a look of sleepy arousal in his eyes, before quickly pulling the bikini cup back over her breast and smoothing the fishnet covering back over her.

When the car stopped, they sat primly side by side holding hands, like two innocent schoolkids at the end of a field trip. They nodded politely to the guy, still chomping on the cigar butt, smiled to the ticket taker.

Once they were out of earshot, Bill tugged her closer.

"The Ferris wheel is not only my favorite ride," he murmured, nuzzling his chin on her head, "it's now my favorite fantasy, too."

7

SEVERAL HOURS LATER, after hooking up with Matt and Candy, and Sara and Drew, at the Hot Shot Photo contest booth, and everyone getting the text number for downloading photos, Ellie and Bill had meandered through the rest of the festival, taking photos, noshing on pretzels and later cotton candy, but mostly enjoying each other's company.

Night had fallen. Overhead, stars littered the dark sky. In the distance, lights of homes dotted the Santa Monica Mountains. Party hounds, tanned and laughing, were heading to some of the beach hot spots for drinks and more festival games.

Ellie and Bill paused in front of a fenced-in area with a dance floor. Over the gate was a sign, in bright pink and purple letters, Good Vibrations Contest, Wednesday, 7:00 p.m.

Ellie, her lips moving as she silently read the rules, suddenly laughed.

"Listen to this," she said. "'How good, good, good can you be to the tune "Good Vibrations"? You can be a dancing maniac, a juggler, a mime, just be good!

Contestants will be judged on ingenuity, creativity, and ability to keep the beat. Sexy, yes! X-rated, no! We'll play the Beach Boys hit version, or bring your own! Couples win double the points!'"

"Thinking of entering?" asked Bill.

"Maybe. I've raked in points by being hired as an extra, thank you very much, then nailed more points at Truth or Bare. Maybe some of the photos you and I downloaded from the Ferris wheel might place, but meanwhile, I should find other contests to enter, try and pull in more points for Team Java Mammas."

She was already planning how she'd spend the rest of the week without Bill, which saddened her.

"Good Vibrations, huh?" He scanned the rules. "What are you thinking of doing?"

"Have no idea."

"I have an idea. Play on your Queen of Evil tattoo."

At first she wanted to laugh, but maybe he was onto something. She thought about some of the dressier clothes she'd packed. "I have a burlesque skirt. If I give it a good tug, the Queen of Evil will show." She paused, wondering if that came out the way it was meant.

"You do burlesque?"

"No, it's a style of skirt. Although I've seen Dita Von Teese do burlesque. YouTube has videos of her performances, some Burlesque 101 stuff, too. I could watch them, copy a few moves."

"Dita Von Who?"

"Von Teese. She was married to Marilyn Manson."

"That shock-rock guy?"

She nodded.

He gave his head a disbelieving shake. "He looks like *Night of the Living Dead* who needs some serious makeup rehab. I didn't even know he dated women."

So not funny. She could take the time to explain Marilyn Manson's performances were tongue-in-cheek, but why bother? Bottom line, just as he'd never understand or appreciate Lou Reed, or the girls from the hood with their tats and makeup, he'd never accept her lifestyle, either.

All the more reason to stick with the midnight cutoff.

"Bill!" called out a male voice.

Jimmie came jogging up to them. "Glad I found you." He stopped, catching his breath. "Would've called, but my cell ran out of power." He nodded hello to Ellie, turned back to Bill. "Hey, Sullivan hates the setting for the first shoot, wants a new location."

Bill muttered an expletive.

"I know. He always does this. Figured you'd want to know before you got a big surprise tomorrow at 5:00 a.m."

"Sullivan's a micromanaging idiot."

"True. But he's our micromanaging idiot boss, unfortunately."

Bill blew out an exasperated breath. "Gordon's given me directorial power over the next few days, including final approval on all locations, to test my wings. Sullivan's last-minute bullshit could not only screw things up, but make me look bad."

Jimmie put his hand on Bill's shoulder. "I know, man. If you want to try and talk sense to Sullivan, he'll be back at his trailer in an hour."

"I'll be there."

Jimmie smiled. "That's the spirit. Hate to run, but promised the wife I'd let some guy named Majello read our brains."

"Thanks for finding me."

Jimmie smiled. "You'll handle this, Bill, just as you handle everything. You're going to be a director, whether it's on this shoot or elsewhere…." He gave his pal a knowing look. "I tell ya, indie film companies are the way to go. I'd even let you have top billing. BillJim Productions."

Bill grinned, his dark cloud lifting. "Get outta here. Bev's waiting."

With a wave, Jimmie jogged away.

Bill looked at Ellie. "Sorry."

"Work happens. I understand."

"So…where were we?"

The night air floated around them, bringing with it scents of corn dogs and the ocean. Nearby, people laughed and clapped at one of the ongoing games. It had been fun, a day to remember, but it was over.

"It's time to go home," she said softly.

"Yeah, appears that way, doesn't it?" He scratched his chin. "Your beach house is nearby?"

"Fifteen-minute walk, but you have your meeting—"

"No. A gentleman escorts his date home, and that's what I'm doing. Besides…"

"What?"

He ran his hand down her arm, looked deeply into her eyes. That's all it took, a touch and a look, and she felt her body go weak with wanting. For all her mental calculations on the pros and the cons of what they were doing, or what he'd think if he knew the truth, sometimes what was going on between them boiled down to something hot and needy that had nothing to do with the mind, and everything to do with the body.

"Like you need to ask," he murmured huskily, linking his fingers with hers. "C'mon, I'm walking you home."

ALMOST FIFTEEN MINUTES later, they stood on the porch of the beach house. Down by the shore, some diehards were boogie boarding, squeezing the very last moments out of the day. From a nearby beach house, the sultry beat of an old Doors tune, "Light My Fire," was playing.

Bill stepped closer. "Sorry."

"For?"

"Not being able to stay and light your fire."

"It's okay."

"No, it's not. I wanted to make love with you…"
He trailed a finger down the side of her face, then

played with her hair. "How about our moving that midnight cutoff to tomorrow night?"

His musky, cinnamon cologne was wreaking havoc with her thought processes. It was shadowy under the porch awning, although the lamp highlighted the lower half of his face. It was impossible to decipher the look in his dark eyes, although she felt him watching her, waiting for an answer.

Now was the time. Just say it.

"We're so different," she began.

He gave a so-what shrug. "But in some ways, we're the same."

She hadn't expected that. "Such as?"

"We both appreciate those classic films of Hollywood's Golden Age. We like to hang out in security guard shacks and eat their food. C'mon, how are we so different that you can't see me tomorrow night?"

"I didn't say that!"

"But you were starting to."

"Okay." She paused. "I like Marilyn Manson." She was wussing out, but considering he'd be leaving any moment, she didn't want to hit him with the fact she'd been faking the whole beach babe bit all day long. Instead, she'd test the waters, let him know that something he laughed at, she respected.

He reared back his head slightly. "You don't say."

"I say."

He lowered his head, barely suppressing a chuckle. He met her gaze. "I put my foot into it, didn't I?"

"Yes."

"He's really straight?"

"Yes."

"I shouldn't have made that comment. Sorry."

His honesty could sometimes be disarming. And charming.

"But you have to admit, Ellie, the guy can sure dress weird."

"What's weird to some might be creative and artistic to others."

He paused. "Well said. I'm sorry I said he looks like—"

"*Night of the Living Dead* who needs some serious makeup rehab."

"I'm impressed you remember verbatim." He cleared his throat, made a two-fingered Boy Scout sign. "I won't make any more disparaging remarks about Marilyn Manson, you have my word."

"Thank you."

He blew out a long breath. "Now that that's covered, what about tomorrow night?"

She smiled. "Yes, let's get together."

"Good, because if you'd said no," he warned, his husky voice tinged with mirth, "I'd have come back anyway." He checked his watch. "I need to leave in a minute. But before I go, about tomorrow on the set. It's going to be crazy busy for me because I'll be stepping into the director's seat, but I'll try to catch up with you."

"Thanks for letting me know."

He slowly fisted the fishnet material in his hand

and pulled her toward him, his eyes darkening to the shade of a moonless midnight.

She came willingly, until she stood mere inches from him, so close she could feel the heat radiating off his body.

He released his grip, dropping both hands to her hips. He kneaded them slowly as he released a strangled groan, then moved his hands around, cupping her buttocks and pulling her closer.

"Kiss me," he murmured, his words puffing warm against her mouth.

She slid her arms up his chest, around his neck, and rose up on tiptoe. Angling her head slightly, she slanted her mouth on his, their lips almost touching.

But she didn't kiss him.

She pressed her bikini top against his chest and rubbed her breasts against him, once, twice, until she felt her nipples go hard.

"Do you feel that?" she whispered against his mouth.

He released a strangled "Yes."

She liked feeling her sexual power, knowing she was exciting him, giving him something to remember until tomorrow night. Pressing her groin against his erection, she moved against him with small, tight circular motions.

"Do you like that?"

His voice cracked as he spoke. "Yes."

"I like it, too," she murmured, pressing her lips against his.

His lips were firm but full, and incredibly, deliciously soft. She moved her mouth against his in a slow, sweeping movement, her lips nibbling, sliding, pecking. She was so excited, her entire body was shaking, her breaths ragged, but she wanted more, now, because this was all she was going to get tonight.

A moan escaped her mouth as she eased her tongue between his lips. He tasted like cotton candy and lemonade, sweet and citrusy. She swept the warm, wet cavern of his mouth with slow, broad strokes, then, with a light flick, coyly teased his tongue to come play.

With a low, guttural sound, he jerked her closer, invading her mouth with his. His hard legs sandwiched on either side of hers, he ground his erection against her sex as his mouth made love to hers, his tongue tangling and sliding and licking at a frantically building pace, until, with a loud moan, he jerked back his head, ripping free from the kiss.

For a long moment, they stood stock-still except for their heaving chests, holding each other at an arm's length.

"If that's just a kiss," he muttered, "I'm dog meat."

8

ELLIE LEANED AGAINST the other side of the closed front door, her eyes closed. That was, unequivocally, the best kiss she'd ever experienced. Ever.

She ran her tongue over her lips, tasting Bill again. Warm and sweet. And the barest trace of citrus.

She opened her eyes and looked around Team Java Mamma's beach pad. "Sara? Candy?"

No answer.

She raised her voice. "I can't believe you guys! I'm ready to spill about the steamiest kiss I've ever had, and you're not here!"

Silence.

"Your loss."

She pushed off from the door and walked like a zombie toward her bedroom. What she'd planned for this vacation had turned upside down. Instead of hanging out in the beach house all day and wandering out at night, she was doing the exact opposite.

She turned a corner and shrieked.

As did the woman who faced her.

Ellie paused, her mouth still open.

As was the woman's.

"Jeez," she whispered, staring at her reflection, "you scared me." She blew out a breath. "I've got to remember this mirror is here, or I'll be shrieking all week long."

Calmer, she checked out her made-over self. Tousled, blond-streaked hair had replaced the black spikes. Tanned skin had replaced the pale look. And those pastels—light green on her lids, peach on her cheeks—had replaced the bright blues and decadent reds.

She stopped by her bedroom, looked around. Its white rattan furniture, sea-foam green walls and tropical print curtains were the antithesis of her antique furniture, Victorian wallpaper and red velvet drapes back home. Seemed everything in her immediate world had been made over. She flashed back to tonight when they'd all hooked up at the Hot Shot booth. Even her brother, Matt, had been made over!

She felt too keyed up to sleep so she decided to get ready for bed, then listen to that CD Tish gave her, a surf-goth group called Vampire Girls on the Beach. If Ellie recalled correctly, they'd done a cover of "Good Vibrations."

As she was fishing in her suitcase for her Siouxsie Sioux T-shirt, which doubled as her jammies, she ran across a girl's best friend.

Her favorite vibrator, OhMiBod, and its trusty sidekick, the wireless remote.

No more frustration for this girl!

She kicked off her shoes, whipped off her clothes and slithered into OhMiBod, adjusting its elastic bands over her hips so the butterfly-shaped vibrator sat *right there* over her clit. After slipping on her long T-shirt, she grabbed the Vampire Girls on the Beach CD, and looked around for her CD player.

Not here. She headed down the hall, checked the bathroom, finally found it in the living room. Cool. Considering she forgot to bring her headphones, she'd have to hook it up to the speakers in here.

In her West L.A. apartment, she could use her OhMiBod wherever she pleased, but the living room in this beach house was communal property.

She crossed to the front door and locked the dead bolt. Problem solved. As it could only be opened from the inside, by her, she could enjoy her OhMi-Bod without a worry.

She slipped on the CD and selected the "Good Vibrations" cut. Not bad. An interesting mix of fifties' surfer music with a dark, pulsing undertone. She preferred bands like Siouxsie & the Banshees and The Cure, although goth-surf music had its pluses. She bobbed her head in time to the music.

She fingered the remote, an ivory plastic device with three speeds and four pulsations, which made any woman a masturbation maestro. If she wanted to enjoy a classical experience, low speed with a slower pulse. Jazzy, medium speed with a higher pulse. Rock and roll? Full speed ahead and max the pulse, baby!

Surf-goth was a more classical experience, she decided. She pressed the buttons.

A light, incessant buzzing quivered against her clit. She sucked in a breath, giving herself over to the delicious sensations. She'd endured hours of foreplay today with Bill. All that teasing and taunting and touching had made her one worked-up, strapped-on, ready-for-relief woman.

She eased down onto a chair, leaned back her head and closed her eyes. She imagined herself at this morning's audition again, alone on the stage, wearing nothing but the OhMiBod and those stilettos. In the audience was one man, Bill, who'd paid her to pleasure herself as he watched. With one caveat. She had to share her fantasy, down to the most minute detail, as it unfolded in her mind.

She spread her legs, imagining him sitting in the very first row. His dark eyes glistened, a look of hunger on his face, as he waited to hear her innermost secrets....

Ding dong.

She snapped open her eyes. Oh, great. Somebody was at the frickin' door.

With an exasperated huff, she punched off the remote. She stood, smoothed down her T-shirt so it hit midthigh, then shuffled to the door and peered through the peephole.

Her heart leaped into her throat.

Bill!

She hated to be caught in the act. It was an insult,

wasn't it, for a guy to find a woman he'd just left to be in the throes of masturbation?

No sweat. He didn't have to know what she'd been doing.

Opening the door slightly, holding the remote in her out-of-sight hand, she said a bit breathlessly, "Hi."

He held out her cell phone. "Figured you'd be needing this before tomorrow night. Forgot I had it on me."

"Thanks." With her free hand, she accepted it.

He cocked his head. "That's 'Good Vibrations,' isn't it?"

She nodded.

"Never heard that version before. Practicing for tomorrow night?"

She tightened her grip on the remote. "Sort of."

"Since we're getting together, how about if we both enter? Double the points for Java Mambo?"

"Java Mammas."

"Right." He flashed her a smile. "I'm feeling a little odd with a door between us."

"Oh, sorry." She opened it a bit wider, still keeping the remote out of view. "Thought you needed to leave right away again, you know, to see that producer."

"I can walk there in ten minutes, and he's not expected for at least twenty, so I have a few minutes to spare."

He leaned his head close to hers and gave her a

smile that warmed her right down to her beach babe peach-tipped toes.

She smiled back, her insides turning to mush.

He leaned closer and brushed his lips across hers, igniting a flame that spread like wildfire over her skin.

"I have a confession to make," she whispered.

"Hmm?"

She handed him the remote.

9

BILL PEERED at the remote in his hand. "What's this for?"

"How soon do you have to leave?" she whispered, opening the door a little wider.

"Five minutes?"

She smiled, excited at the thoughts searing through her wanton mind. She glanced over his shoulder, not seeing anyone for several hundred feet, either on the walkway or the beach. With Bill blocking her, no one could see her…and if she saw anyone, she could quickly duck back inside.

She lifted the end of her T-shirt, brushed her fingers across the elastic over her hip, leading his eyes down to the object positioned over her sex.

He looked down, paused. "God, you're so pretty," he murmured. "Is that what I think it is?"

"Yes."

Raising his gaze, he held up the object. "And this is…"

"A remote."

"Well, well, well…" He held it inside the door to

read the buttons. "Aren't you the electronic-age wonder."

"I'd invite you inside," she whispered, "but selfishly, I'd like to stand right here...."

His eyes glistened with lust. "I wanted to make love the first time, not just..."

She stealthily rubbed her thighs together in anticipation. "Let's call this an appetizer before the main meal."

He leaned forward, his breath warm against her neck. "Appetizer, yes...I like that." Fastening his lips on her neck, he lightly nibbled and kissed, causing her to writhe pleasurably.

Then he pulled back and looked at her. "I'm selfish, too," he said, positioning his finger on a button, "because I want to watch."

He pressed a button that brought Ellie onto her toes, the exquisite tremors zeroing right in on her sex. So intensely enjoyable, all it would take was a few more moments and she'd...

Bill stared at the hem of her T-shirt that fluttered with breezes over the firm, creamy skin of her thighs. She was rising up on her toes, pressing together her lips to suppress the needy mewling noises that lodged in her throat.

It was dark enough on the porch that it'd be difficult for someone to see unless they were standing in his shoes, plus his body blocked her....

"Lift your T-shirt," he murmured, "I want to see you."

She reached down and lifted it.

"Ellie…" He pressed another button and she gasped. "I can't wait to taste you…touch you…."

Panting, she opened her eyes and looked at him, her hips rocking slightly. "More," she said on a moan. "I want more."

Ellie felt the vibrations kick up a notch. She gasped as sheer, exacting need pooled hotly between her legs. The pleasure was so intense, so exquisite, she throbbed and ached for release from the soles of her feet to the top of her head as the tension kept building, building….

Her breath caught as her body tightened and trembled. She was hot, wet, wound so tight. Her body needed it, demanded it…so close….

For a singular moment, everything stilled…then her entire being rushed toward the point of no return….

She bit back a groan as wave after wave of release ripped through her until, too shaky to keep standing, she slumped her lax, sated body into Bill's arms.

He dropped the remote as he held her close, her breaths warm and ragged against his cheek as her body relaxed into his embrace.

Suddenly, she sputtered a soft laugh. "I think I just proved that old saying wrong."

"What saying?"

"Never come between a man and his remote? Well, I think I just did."

THE FOLLOWING MORNING, at 8:00 a.m. sharp, Ellie reported to the assistant casting director, Peter, on the set of *Sin on the Beach.* She'd met Peter the day before at her audition, so she wasn't surprised at his whirl of frenetic energy—chain-smoking, drinking coffee, ordering people around, all while talking into his cell.

She stood nearby, waiting for him to end his call. This morning, before getting ready, she'd had coffee with Sara and Candy, but despite their guy-talk tell-all, she'd stayed mum about what had happened last night with Bill. Oh, she'd said she and Bill had *kissed,* but hadn't breathed a word about the orgasm-in-the-doorway escapade. They would have loved hearing about Ellie's crazy-hot encounter, but she liked keeping it private, something shared between her and Bill only.

"You!" Peter pointed at her with his cigarette, the other hand holding his cell to his ear. "I thought I said no black bikinis!"

She started to stutter something, when he cut her off.

"Next time follow directions." He made a hold-it gesture while barking into the phone, "I don't care what he says! It's Thursday or nothing, darling." He looked up at Ellie, pointing her to a group of people in bikinis and shorts.

She headed over to the group of ten or so people, whom she assumed were her fellow extras. The girls all looked like Paris Hilton, the guys like Brad Pitt, which made the older gentleman in red shorts and a T-shirt that read Surfers Stay on Longer stand out.

Probably because she kept staring at him, he approached her with the kind of pickup line that was right up her alley.

"Want a cup of coffee?" he asked.

His long sideburns and handlebar mustache were a throwback to another era. Reminded her of herself, modeling her glam style on stars of yesteryear. The two of them obviously marched to their own stylistic drummers, which put her instantly at ease with him.

"No thanks." She smiled. "Afraid I'm picky. I run a coffee shop."

He lit up. "Well, isn't this a small world. My grandson's new friend is rooming with someone who runs a coffee shop."

A few pieces fell into place. "Your grandson wouldn't happen to run a surf shop, would he?"

"Why, yes!"

"Yes, it's a very small world." She held out her hand. "I'm Sara's friend Ellie, the one who runs a coffee shop."

He shook her hand. "Pleased to meet you. I'm Gus."

They spent the next few minutes chatting about the surf shop, her coffee shop, Gus's past surfing accomplishments. She didn't take his flirting seriously. In fact, if he were forty years younger, and she weren't besotted with Bill, she might've said yes…to a coffee date.

"Hey," said a familiar voice.

Bill.

Her heart shoved into overdrive. "Hey, yourself."

Gus gave a little salute and wandered off, leaving the two of them alone.

"Should I be jealous?" Bill teased.

Ellie looked over at Gus, who was already flirting with another extra. "No, I'm already a thing in his past."

Bill grinned. "Gotta get ready for the next take, so can't stay long, but would you like to have lunch together? Wait, let me clarify that. When the set breaks for lunch, would you like to take a walk on the beach while eating whatever I can get delivered? With my busy schedule, that's the best I can do."

"Love to," she said. "Where?"

"Just come over to my station." He pointed to an oversize blue-and-white striped umbrella, under which were several canvas-backed chairs, a portable video monitor, a small table on which sat a laptop, some papers.

She smiled. "Sounds great."

"Bill!" A red-haired kid wearing a *Sin on the Beach* T-shirt and blue baggy shorts barged in. "Video feed is having problems. Kenny needs to see you ASAP."

Bill touched her arm. "Gotta go. By the way, you look great."

"Sorry I wore black," she said, but he was already walking away. Even as he talked to the red-haired kid, others kept approaching him, vying for his attention. The boy from the hood had certainly come a long way. Even back then, he'd had that cocky, I'm-the-man way about him, which a guy had to have to stand up to, and often survive, the life on the streets. She wondered if he'd even have come this far if he hadn't had that tough background.

And yet, he seemed to despise the past that had nurtured this success. She didn't get it.

OVER THE NEXT THREE HOURS, what Ellie *did* get was that the film business was no way as glitzy behind the scenes as it was on the screen. The next several hours consisted of boredom, repetition and more boredom as the same scene—two people having a brief conversation—was shot again and again.

At eleven the assistant director instructed everyone to take thirty minutes for lunch, and she headed over to Bill's station, which was a mob scene with people demanding his time. She stood outside the umbrella while he argued with a lighting guy, gave instructions to several others, handled a call from Sullivan, all the while watching a playback on the video monitor of the scene they'd just shot.

Seemed it wasn't just Peter who multiprocessed on this set.

She was debating whether to walk away, when the crowd dispersed and Bill waved her into his inner sanctum.

"Sorry," he said, standing. "Today's been one problem after another." He picked up a sack, nudged his head toward the beach. "Let's get the hell out of Dodge."

Minutes later, they strolled along the shore, their

feet sinking into the wet sand. Overhead, seagulls squawked and circled, eager for any offerings.

"It's one of the worst shoots I've ever been on," Bill muttered, shaking his head. "Just my luck, it's also the first day with *me* in the director's chair proving myself."

She munched her sandwich, listening.

"But let's not ruin our lunch by discussing it anymore, okay?"

"It's great being on the beach," she said, watching the distant waves tumble and crash.

"Yeah, except the majestic Pacific is starting to look like the damn show to me, but you're right. It's great out here. Hey, it was also great to see your brother again last night. What's he doing these days?"

"Vice president at a software company."

Bill nodded approvingly. "Not surprised one bit. He was always a go-getter." He took a swig of his soda.

"How about your brothers and sisters?"

Bill felt that familiar nagging discomfort when people started talking about families. "They're all right."

His cell phone rang. Juggling his sandwich and drink, he retrieved it from his shirt pocket, checked the caller ID. "It can wait," he muttered, dropping the phone back into his pocket. "So where were we?"

"I was asking about your family."

He paused. "You know something, Ellie? Even though we laughed and talked about Olvera Street yesterday, the truth is, I hate East L.A. I know, you love it. Or at least like it. Why, I'll never understand, but you do." He took a bite of his sandwich, stared off at the ocean as he chewed.

"Sorry," she said softly.

He took another swig of soda, taking his time to swallow the cold, fizzy liquid. "No, I'm sorry," he said. "I meant what I said—I don't understand—but I could've been a nice guy and not a…"

She lightly touched his arm, her kindness making him feel even more like a jerk.

"Jasmine works in a hair salon," he started out, "has two kids, still lives in the hood. The next oldest, Sabrina, dropped out her sophomore year. Tried to talk her out of it, but…" He shrugged. "She's divorced, several kids, living with Mom in a condo a few blocks over from our old hood.

"My brother Jasper," he continued, staring down the beach at a couple of kids flying a bright blue and yellow kite, "is a firefighter in Eugene, Oregon."

"That's a beautiful town. Summer after high school, my girlfriends and I did a road trip to Washington state. We stopped in Eugene on the way back."

"Yeah, I visited Jasper while on a shoot there. He's happily married, *four* kids. Wife's getting her master's in psychology." He finished the last bite of his sandwich.

"And your youngest brother?"

Suddenly the breezy summer air grew hotter,

thicker. The glare of the sun on water hurt his eyes. This was the tough one, the one he never discussed.

"Wasn't his name Randall?" she asked.

"Reginald." He paused, picked up a shell embedded in the wet sand. "We called him Reggie."

"Right! Reggie." She smiled. "Once he came over to show off a mitt that'd been signed by—"

"Fernando Valenzuela. Dodgers' pitcher." Bill tossed the shell into the ocean, watched it disappear into the swirl of water and foam. "When he was eleven, all he talked about was being the next Fernando."

"What is he doing now?"

Bill watched where the shell had dropped, wondering if it had sunk to the bottom or was drifting out to sea.

"He died," he said matter-of-factly. "Gang shooting. Drive-by. Bloods and Crips, same old trash, what can I say."

He looked over at Ellie, wondering about the expression in her eyes, hidden behind those sunglasses. Did she feel pity for him? Sadness? Definitely not forgiveness because if he couldn't feel that for himself, neither could anybody else.

He looked back at the set. "We need to go. I bet twenty people are looking for me, ready to pound me with questions and problems."

"Wait a minute, Bill," she murmured, moving closer. He automatically braced himself as she wrapped her arms around him. "I'm so sorry," she whispered.

He didn't want this. Didn't want her touching

him, feeling bad for him, saying empty words that would never bring Reggie back.

But even as he thought those things, he reached for her, his hand trailing down the jut of her hip, onto the soft material of her bikini. Her warmth, her caring, even her screwed-on-wrong beliefs awakened something in him that made him want to feel again.

He held her close, feeling her soft body against his, needing that softness, craving it. The weight he'd carried for so long suddenly felt too heavy, too much to endure alone. He lowered his head, letting it sink against the cushion of her perfumed hair. He was so tired of keeping it all together, so tired of holding back.

"Ellie," he whispered hoarsely, "it's my fault he died."

10

LATER THAT AFTERNOON, what had been *one* of the worst shoots Bill had ever been on, became *the* worst.

"Have you lost your effing mind?" He paced a few feet, eyeing the video monitor. It was stifling hot, the stench of exhaust from Pacific Coast Highway overpowered the sea air, some know-nothing had just sabotaged a perfect take, and to make the day as perfect as it could possibly be, he'd lost his watch somewhere in miles of sand.

It was as though the universe was saying, "Have a crappy day."

He stopped, pointed at the monitor again. "The lighting sucked! Our star was in shadow, but the lifeguard station was lit up like Disneyland!"

The chief gaffer, a glop of sunscreen on his nose, nodded. "Yes, Bill. Sorry. Won't happen again."

Bill rubbed a spot on his chin. "Yeah, okay, I'm sorry I'm being a dick. It's just that it's—" He looked over at one of the production assistants. "What time is it?"

The girl, her pile of red hair pinned to the top of her head with a clip, glanced nervously at her watch. "It's 2:30 p.m."

"Nearly three," he sputtered under his breath. He looked back at the gaffer. "You hear that? It's nearly 3:00 p.m.! We've been shooting since 5:00 a.m., and we're *still* screwing up the *first* frickin' scene."

He stretched his neck from side to side, trying to dislodge the kink that had homesteaded between his blades, as he walked out onto the set where everyone could see him. He stopped, looked over the assembly of crew and actors.

"People," he called out, "can we pull together and finally, *finally,* get it right this next time? Otherwise, we'll have wasted an entire day with nothing to show for it."

"Yes."

"Sure thing, Bill."

"Will do."

His gaze caught Jimmie's, who stood with several of his reports. Even under a glaring sun, Bill could tell that look on his pal's face. They all needed a time-out before Bill went postal.

He signaled to the second assistant director, a quiet kid everyone called Bunker for some reason, and flashed five splayed fingers.

Bunker nodded, raised the megaphone to his lips.

"Everybody, take five. Be back in your places at exactly two-thirty-five. No excuses."

Bill grabbed his bottle of iced tea and took a long

swig as he watched Jimmie trudge through the sand toward him.

"I don't get it," Bill said when his friend arrived, glancing down at Jimmie's expensive leather huaraches. "Why do you get involved with this bullshit? Why don't you stay at home and write full-time, skip this insanity. You have the means."

"Cheap shot, Bill."

"Sorry. Maybe I should change my name to Dick so people can call me that to my face." He looked around at people adjusting lights, dragging equipment across the sand, fixing the stars' melting make-up. Typically, people would be chatting, yelling, cracking jokes.

Except for the occasional murmur of conversation, everyone was stone-cold silent.

"I'm making everybody tense."

"Yeah, you are, but it's also a tough shoot."

"Starting with Sullivan this morning." Bill was still angry at the producer's bullheadedness. "He insisted the location shot be moved, so it was moved. That cost time, money and one pissed-off star's goodwill because no one told her the site of the new location."

"Shoots happen."

"Very funny."

"C'mon, Bill, you and I both know it's a crazy business."

"But not on the first day of the most important shoot of my career."

"This is one step above a sitcom, Bill. Lots of bodies and fluff, barely enough plot to string along a story line—"

"Getting ready to hawk the indie film company again?"

"BillJim Productions? Whose first film has an award-winning script featuring a compelling and complex protagonist based on your life?" He paused. "No. That's a lost cause."

"The money would suck."

"Not if you'd stop thinking making it big equates to making big bucks. But I don't want to discuss it further."

Bill grunted. "Me, neither. Except to say, you'd be smart to contract with that financial guy who used to work for Coppola—Gary something—because he knows the business end inside and out."

"Gary Minger. Had lunch with him last week."

Bill paused. "Did you pitch him the indie film company idea?"

"Thought we weren't discussing this further."

"We're not."

"Great, let's change the subject. How's our Queen of Evil?"

A smile broke through Bill's black mood. "Fine."

"Fine?"

"Okay, extra fine. She's…good, you know?"

He thought about how his heart pounded every time she smiled. And how he'd told her about Reggie. It hadn't been easy, but he was glad now he'd done it. She was more than a lover. She'd become his friend.

Bill dragged a hand through his tangle of hair. "Have you ever listened to Marilyn Manson?"

Jimmie did a double take. "That strange guy? Never. Plan to keep it that way."

"He's okay."

"Uh, why are we talking about Marilyn Manson?"

"Oh, Ellie likes him."

"Seeing her again?"

"Tonight."

Jimmie nodded. "Give it a chance before you pull the plug. A relationship—that's dating someone for more than three months, by the way—with the right person might do you good. Help you get outside of yourself, give your life some perspective. Can't be number one all the time, Bill. Unless you like living in that small, lonely place."

"Giving me some tough love, James?"

"If I don't, who will?" He made a power sign, bumped it against Bill's fist. "Gotta check on the grips. I know how you love the details, but try not to sweat the small stuff, okay?"

"I'll try."

BUT A HALF HOUR LATER, Bill wasn't just sweating the small stuff, he was sweating the minutiae, too.

He stood, his arms crossed, staring down a group of extras. Dressed in Speedos and bikinis, their tanned bodies glistening with lotion, they stared back with wide, frightened eyes as though he was going to yell "boo!" any moment.

Except for the old guy in surfer trunks, who was taking advantage of the break to make eyes at one of the female props personnel.

"Who didn't turn off their cell phone?" Bill demanded, his voice rolling over the quiet set.

Overhead, a plane buzzed slowly through the blue, trailing an advertising sign that read Rocko's Burgers Best in Malibu 1-800-555-6609.

Peter, the assistant casting director, sat stiffly on the edge of the set, lighting another cigarette. "People," he said, half puffing the words as they escaped in a plume of smoke, "the director just asked you a question."

Not the director, yet. After this last screwup, maybe never.

An hour ago, Sullivan, who'd spent most of the day watching the taping from his producer's trailer, had taken Bill aside. In a buddy-buddy tone, he'd calmly reviewed the day. Costly. Mistakes happen. Did Bill want Gordon to take over the directing? No? Then, could Bill please get back control of the set and stop the bleeding?

That last shot hadn't just bled, it'd gushed.

In the group of extras, a woman stepped forward, her head bent. "It was me," she said meekly, lifting her gaze.

Ellie.

She nervously clasped and unclasped her hands,

the look on her face so damn remorseful, he almost felt bad. Almost. The next chat with Sullivan wasn't going to be so buddy-buddy.

Peter, taking another puff, strode up to her.

"You were explicitly told to leave your cell back at the extras' table." Although he stood right directly in front of her, he spoke loud enough so everyone could hear. "You're fired. Pick up your things and—"

"Hold it!" Bill pulled off his headset and rubbed his thumb and forefinger against his eyelids. After a moment, he lowered his hand, took a breath. "There's enough drama in front of the cameras, do we have to have it behind the cameras, too?"

Somebody snickered.

He looked at Ellie, still standing in the spot where she'd confessed, looking frightened and vulnerable.

Despite his pissed-off state, he felt for her.

"Let's not go to extremes, Peter." Bill motioned to the production assistant to hand him his tea. "She's not a professional. She's just somebody who won this job at the festival audition. Let her stay. *Minus* her cell, of course."

While Peter divested Ellie of her phone, Bill returned to his station, sipping lukewarm tea while waiting for the camera operators to give him their thumbs-up. Patience had never been one of his better traits. He liked things done fast, well and on time, but he could dream on wanting that on this set. He ticked off the seconds in his head, nudged his toe into the warm sand and waited.

Seconds became minutes.

A pair of pink polished toes entered his line of vision. He looked up.

Ellie stood there, guilt so clearly etched on her sun-pink face, she might as well carry a sign.

"I'm really, really sorry," she whispered, her voice shaking.

He watched her through slitted eyes. Over the years, he'd dealt with all kinds, from hard-assed gang-bangers to scheming studio heads. He'd been hassled and manipulated and tested by the best, but he'd usually been able to keep his attitude on cruise control.

But he was having a hell of a time doing that today. As wonderful as she was, as much as she meant to him, she'd just pricked his balloon of dreams with a very sharp needle.

He shifted in his chair, his face hot, his heart hammering, every single nerve ending raw, edgy, inflamed as years of scrambling for jobs, living on little sleep and food, fighting to prove himself rose to the surface.

He kept his eyes fixed on her face, all too aware of her plump breasts, smooth thighs and the sweet triangle nestled in between.

Part of him wanted to curse her, make her the scapegoat for this rotten day, for his rapidly down-hill-sliding career, for every single piece of malfunctioning equipment, misspoken dialogue, hell, even for the script assistant's summer cold.

The other part wanted to crush her into his arms and ride her right into the ground.

"You're making me crazy, Ellie," he muttered.

Over her shoulder he saw Ricardo, one of the continuity crew, heading his way. Ricardo was a can-do kinda guy who resolved problems before anyone else even knew they existed.

Which meant one big, hairy, unmanageable problem was heading Bill's way.

Turning to pick up his drink, he realized Ellie was still standing there, an expectant look on her face.

"What?" he barked.

She gave a little jump. "I, uh, was wondering…"

He took a sip, waited for the rest. "C'mon, I don't have time to play guess what's on my mind."

Now she looked hurt.

He squeezed his eyes shut. "Sorry, sorry, I don't mean to be an asshole. Just spit it out. Company's on its way."

"I was wondering if I could leave—"

"Bil-ly…" Phoebe strolled in, wearing a skimpy summer dress that was more skimp than dress. She deigned a glance at Ellie, then handed him a paper. "Curtiss asked if you'd read this memo. He needs an answer ASAP."

He took it, started reading.

Phoebe sidled closer. "Going to the festival tonight?"

"Huh? I don't know."

Ricardo stepped into the shade from the tent, wiping the sweat off his chin. "Hey, Bill, sorry to be the messenger, but props brought the wrong motorcycle…."

Bill's cell rang. He made a time-out gesture to Ricardo as he answered, listened to someone start explaining why one of the special effects had prematurely blown up.

"Hold on," he said into the phone. He handed back the memo to Phoebe, "Tell Curtiss the budget's too tight. And about that motorcycle..." He looked over at Ricardo but his gaze froze on Ellie.

"Thought you wanted to leave."

She flitted a glance at the others, looked back. "I, uh..."

"Look," he said, working to keep his voice even, "if you're worried about Peter, I'll talk to him."

"No, it's..."

He didn't have the time for this. "Ellie, I can't waste my time on an *extra*. Go, *leave!* The rest of us have real work to do here."

The aquamarine eyes turned glacial, giving him a look that made him wish he'd never been born.

"You said you don't mean to be," she said quietly, "but you are."

He frowned. "Don't mean to be what?"

"An asshole."

As she walked away, he felt the world pull back, the sounds of machinery and people on the set reduced to a low buzz, like a fly in another room. Even the crashing surf seemed remote, as though it'd chosen another shore.

It wasn't her words. He'd been called worse. Crazy enough, it wasn't even the job. There'd be problems, he'd be on the line, things would be fixed. Or not.

It was realizing he'd finally committed himself to something more than just him. Something better, bigger. Yet within minutes, he'd managed to slam the door and isolate himself again.

Jimmie was right. He'd made himself number one for so long, he hadn't realized what a small, lonely place it really was.

11

THIRTY MINUTES LATER, Ellie was reliving the last few days. She'd gone from glam goth to beach babe, acted and nearly been fired on a national television show....

And called the man of her dreams an asshole.

To his face.

While others were present.

Wow. Was she having fun or what?

She stopped, squiggled a pattern in the wet sand with her toe, his words replaying in her head. *I can't waste my time on an extra.... Go, leave!* She'd spent the first part of her walk furious and hurt that he'd thought she was a waste of time, feeling totally justified in her response.

Now she was blaming herself for approaching him in the first place. Peter had lectured the extras about no cell phones on the set, then the cameras were rolling, she'd belatedly realized she was holding hers, and tried to position herself so it wouldn't be seen. She'd never forget the sickening feeling when she heard the familiar "Walk on the Wild Side" ringtone jangling, realizing it was her cell....

Dumb, dumb, dumb.

She deserved to be chewed out, maybe even fired, but Bill had stood up for her. She should have left it there, but, no, she got it into her head she needed to apologize in person, which actually went okay, and would have remained okay if some anxious part of her hadn't decided she *had* to know if their date tonight was still on.

So she'd stood there—while he was being crowded with people, problems, phone calls—acting all goofy and nervous and not speaking up and he'd gotten frustrated and…

"Hey!" called out a female voice. "Gotta match?"

She looked over at a group of teens sitting and lying on multicolored beach towels, laughing and talking, a radio playing a soulful Jack Johnson tune. They looked to be fifteen, sixteen tops, most drinking from bottles in paper bags.

A girl, shiny brown hair to her waist, waved what appeared to be an unlit cigarette at Ellie.

"Got a match?"

"Sorry, no," she called back.

That's when she noticed they'd parked themselves right in front of one of the numerous No Smoking, No Drinking signs that dotted this part of the beach.

She smiled, remembering her own teenage rebellion. Except, instead of bikinis and hanging at the beach, she'd worn black and put glitter into her hair. Her glam rock phase that eventually became glam goth. Looking back, she sometimes wondered if it was an escape from her growing responsibilities at home, being an adult to her mother's child.

After chores and homework, she'd lounge in her bedroom, smoking clove cigarettes, listening to David Bowie, Bob Dylan, Lou Reed. To say she was besotted with Lou Reed was an understatement. He epitomized New York, the place Bill had gone, which was the be-all and end-all for her young heart. She'd even stenciled the lyrics to one of Reed's songs on her wall, painting the last words of the chorus—"swoop, swoop, rock, rock"—in fluorescent paint on her ceiling. The song itself was a moving tribute to a long-lost lover, yet it ended with those light, silly words—"swoop, swoop, rock, rock"—which to her had meant that no matter what happened, life was good.

Whenever she'd had a bad day, or was going through a tough time, or just needed to remember that everything would work out, she'd lie on her bed and look up at those words, and feel better.

All of which baffled her mother, and immensely amused her brother, Matt.

Matt!

That's who she needed to talk to. He knew her better than anybody. He'd known Bill in the hood, had chatted with him last night at the Hot Shot booth. Matt could give her advice on this mess she'd gotten herself into.

"What's up, El?" he answered a moment later.

"I think I screwed up. No, I know I did. It's bad."

"Oh."

Like most guys, Matt was pretty much clueless how to respond to a woman broaching an emotional topic. Like a computer, he needed to first process the data before formulating an answer.

"It's about Bill Romero."

"Okay."

"As you know, he and I are—" were? "—romantically close." She looked out at the surfers on their boards, bobbing in the ocean, waiting for a wave. Oh, if only life were so simple. "It's a temporary thing, of course."

"Of course," he said quickly. Too quickly.

Oh, right. He and Candy were doing that sensible-sex thing. Usually, Ellie would take this opportunity to play matchmaker, persuade him Candy was the best thing to ever shake up his world... But, for a change, she needed to put her problems first.

"Okay, here goes." She blew out a nervous breath. "There's a French woman named Vi who wants a more serious relationship with Bill."

"French, eh?"

"You don't have to sound so gleeful. Anyway, that's in limbo."

"What does that mean?"

"They'll be discussing their potential when she gets back from Europe in a few weeks."

He made an ominous-sounding grunt.

"However, my more immediate problem is—" she squeezed shut her eyes "—I called him an asshole."

"Were you drinking?"

Her eyes flew open. "No!"

"Did you have a reason to call him that?"

"At the time, I thought so. Now…I'm not so sure."

"Wow." Pause. "You called him that to his face?"

"Yes." She closed her eyes, envisioning it again. "Actually, I didn't call him an asshole outright. It was more of a virtual name-calling thing."

"Have you spoken since then?"

"No."

Another ominous grunt.

"I should add that right before the asshole part, I'd accidentally brought the entire production to a screeching halt."

"What happened?"

"I took my cell onto the set, after I'd been told not to, and it rang in the middle of a big scene."

"Oh."

"After that, I was almost fired, but Bill stood up for me."

"Then, something happened and you called him an asshole?"

"Yes."

"And you want me to…"

"You know me. You know Bill. Plus you're a guy. Tell me the truth. Do you think I've blown it with Bill?"

"Yes."

"Jeez, couldn't you have paused a little, made me think you needed to think it over first?"

"Sorry, sis. Look, I know you feel bad, but analytically speaking, what is he besides a childhood crush? You have your coffee shop, your friends and family, that alter-life as the mistress of the damned…what does it matter if he stays or if he goes?"

"I'm better than this," she said softly.

"In a way, yeah. On the other hand, maybe he's worth it?"

She took a deep breath of the salt-infused air. When she blew it out, she imagined all her cloudy, confused thoughts being expelled with it. She'd been so caught up in what Bill had meant to her as a girl, did she even know what he meant to her as a woman?

She did.

His strength, passion, striving for success appealed to her because those were the traits she most loved about the hood. It wasn't that others didn't have those, it was that, for too many, those characteristics had been turned inside out. She'd been thinking about what she could do to change that. They were small ideas, but everything began with a small step.

Fundamentally Bill was, in the best way, the heart of the community. Although he didn't realize it.

And until this moment, she hadn't realized she wanted to return there with him. Problem was, that would never happen.

"Thanks, Matt. I'll be going now."

"El, you sound so sad. Is there something I can do to make you feel better?"

"No, it's okay. I should be going now—"

"Wait!"

She paused. "What?"

"'Swoop, swoop, rock, rock.'"

She blinked back sudden emotion. "Matthew Rockwell," she murmured, "you're the coolest bro in the world."

AN HOUR LATER, Ellie sat at one of the stools in the kitchen, halfheartedly doodling clothes designs in her sketch pad. Upon returning to the beach house, she'd rummaged through her bag, panicked she'd forgotten to pack her favorite old Lou Reed T-shirt, which had been washed so many times it felt like a soft binky against her skin. She'd literally yelped with joy when she found it.

Wearing it, unfortunately, just wasn't the same as gazing up at "Swoop, swoop, rock, rock."

"El, what's up?" Candy traipsed in, tossed a bag onto the counter and picked up a piece of leftover rugelach.

"Sketching, making coffee."

"Coffee?" Candy laughed. "Hon, I know you miss Dark Gothic Roast, but it's eighty-something degrees outside! It's lemonade time, girl."

Ellie felt the glue holding her together start to crack. Making coffee had seemed a good way to stay busy, avoid the pity party route. But of all the crazy things, the word *lemonade* threatened to undo her.

"Bill and I—" she cleared her suddenly dry throat "—drank lemonades yesterday."

Candy's eyes filled with concern. "El? What happened?"

Ellie set down her pen. "I almost got fired from *Sin on the Beach.*"

"No," Candy murmured.

Fluttering her hands in a no-big-deal gesture, she slid off the stool. "I'm going to get some coffee."

Candy followed. "El, this is a *vacation,* not a job. You can't get fired, and even if they threatened to, tell them you quit because you have better things to do, like hit the surf, catch some rays, have fun in the sun!"

"I prefer fun under the moon, but I get your drift."

"Did something happen with Bill?

Ellie poured a cup, raised the steaming mug midair and paused. "You're right. It's too hot to drink coffee." She poured the brew down the sink. "Is it too early to have a cocktail?"

"For you, no. For me, yes. I want to be sober when I go networking with Matt."

"Networking?"

Candy picked at the piece of rugelach, avoiding Ellie's eyes. "No big deal. I'm just helping him loosen up."

The front door suddenly swung open.

"Hey, Team Java Mammas!" Sara walked in, smiling, looking relaxed. "I'm not staying long. Just a quick in-and-out to pick up some stuff before I go surfing."

Candy raised an eyebrow. "Quick in-and-out?"

Sara wagged a finger. "You know what I mean."

"Yeah, but it's fun teasing you," said Candy. "Going surfing with Drew?"

Sara nodded, her gaze drifting to Ellie. "Hey, how's our movie star?"

"She almost got fired," Candy said quietly.

Sara frowned. "What happened?"

"My cell phone went off. Brought the entire production to a screaming halt." Ellie headed for the kitchen cabinets. "Did we bring anything gooey, loaded with sugar? I know, *chocolate*. I definitely need chocolate."

"There are more Bomb Pops in the freezer," offered Candy.

"Close enough." She headed to the fridge at the back of the kitchen.

Sarah called out after her, "How're you and—"

The question cut off abruptly. No doubt Sara had just caught Candy's frantic don't-ask signals.

"It's okay, we can say the Bill-word," Ellie answered, returning with a pop and settling back onto her seat. She'd been debating whether to share this with the girls, but oh well…

"By the way, there's a French woman named Vi, short for Viaduct or something like that, in the wings." The sound of sucked-in breaths nearly drowned out the sound of distant waves. "Their relationship is in limbo—that means on hold—and they'll be reviewing it when she gets back from her European vacation." She started peeling off the wrapper.

"A French woman," muttered Candy.

Ellie rolled her eyes. "Tell me about it."

"But," said Sara, "their relationship is on hold."

"True." Like she had any room to complain, she who'd initiated the *at-midnight-our-relationship-turns-into-a-pumpkin* decree. Whatever she and Bill did, if they even got together to do it again, would be over way before Vi jet-setted in for the international liaison symposium.

She tugged off the last of the wrapper. "Supposedly we have a date tonight at seven." Their hot one-nighter that ended at twelve straight up. At some point, she'd thought that cutoff point was a logical way to protect the heart, which now seemed plain dumb. Who in their right mind even used the words *logic* and *heart* in the same sentence?

"That's good, right?" Sara looked at Candy, who shrugged.

"Well, after our tension-filled goodbye on the set…" After Matt, she'd decided not to share the asshole story with anyone else. "I'm not so sure our date's still on."

"Why the tension?" Sara looked so sad, Ellie almost wanted to comfort *her*.

"Because my rising sign doesn't like his moon?" She tossed the wrapper into the trash, missed. "Win some, lose some," she muttered. She licked the pop.

Candy gave Sara a look. "She doesn't want to talk about it."

"I know, but I'll worry about it the rest of the day

if I don't know!" Sara turned to Ellie. "Tell me this much. Did you and Bill talk after that?"

"No."

"Maybe you should call him."

"Or," chimed in Candy, "have Matt call. He knew Bill, right?"

"Don't know his cell number, and even if I did, wouldn't call. Wouldn't want Matt to, either." Ellie licked her pop for a moment, thinking about Bill. "That guy," she finally said, lowering her pop, "can be really critical, domineering, opinionated."

"Love them alpha boys," murmured Candy with a smile, which dropped instantly when she caught the looks on Ellie's and Sara's faces. "Sorry."

"Seems to me," Sara said, "those traits are excellent, if not necessary, for a directing career. Maybe he's trying so hard, it's bringing out his worst...but maybe also his best?"

Bill's face materialized in Ellie's mind, his brown eyes sparking with interest as he listened to something she said, as though nothing else in the world mattered. She loved his laugh. Deep, rich, full of enjoyment. She remembered how protected she'd felt on the Ferris wheel, the heady thrill of kissing at the top of the world, how with him she felt safe to open up, be sexually adventurous. And that wicked little soul patch...oh, mama.

In her childhood fantasies, she'd wanted him to be the first man she'd make love with. She'd grown up, there'd been other men, but deep down, that fantasy had never died. It was as though, through all these years, she'd been waiting for Bill. That their chance meeting this week was some kind of destiny.

She looked at Candy and Sara, smiling at their eager we-gotta-know-what-you're-thinking look on their faces.

Ellie took a lick, smiled. "Sara, you're right on. I was thinking about what was best about him as I walked home. He's a passionate, strong, successful guy. He's also funny, smart, *really* listens to what you have to say, has a great body—" she fanned her face with the pop, making them laugh "—and way too much sex appeal for his own good."

"So," said Sara, "what are you going to do?"

Ellie thought for a moment.

"Girls," she finally said, gesturing with the pop, "Ellie the caretaker is going to take care of herself. So I'm going to do what any smart woman should do with a man like that." She wriggled her eyebrows. "Jump his bones."

12

"SIGNIN' UP for Good Vibrations?" With a sleepy grin, the guy brushed back his long hair.

"Yes…" She squinted at his name tag, nearly lost in his bright tie-dyed shirt. "Tommy." She set the plastic bag, which held her stilettos, onto the table. Until she performed, she'd wear thongs.

"Name?" He poised his pen on the sign-up sheet.

"El—Queen of Evil."

After he wrote it down, he stared at her hair.

"It's a crown," she muttered, pulling up one of her fishnet gloves. Between learning burlesque moves, dyeing her hair black again, and getting dressed, there'd been no time to shop for a costume crown, so she'd made one out of aluminum foil.

"Your face," Tommy continued, "reminds me of a porcelain doll my mom had. White face, dark eyes, red lips. Pretty, like you."

"Thanks." She looked around for Bill. What would she see in his face? Acceptance? Amusement? Disgust?

"Performing as a single or couple?"

"Single. Maybe couple."

Tommy fidgeted with his pen for a moment. "I'm not supposed to do this, but I'll write you down as both, just in case."

"Okay."

After he finished writing, he set down the pen. "Okay, here's the part where I point out where the changing room is—" he pointed to a curtained-off changing area on the far side of the stage "—and I tell you the rules." He started reciting in a monotone. "No alcoholic beverages in the act, no X-rated movements, gestures or words, no…"

She'd already read them. Pretending to listen, she checked out the crowd. Most wore bikinis and swim trunks—spectators, she guessed, with a few who'd signed up on a whim. Some, like her, had obviously prepared. Like the couple in matching red T-shirts, holding identical back massagers. Or the surfer-dude, with Good Vibes painted onto his T-shirt, practicing on his harmonica. The guy pouring water into glasses arranged on a table didn't seem to fit, but the woman in the silver bodysuit, which seemed to vibrate with her every move, was definitely a contender.

She froze.

That vibrating silver woman was *Phoebe.* She'd piled her blond hair into some kind of cone-shaped beehive, wore a push-up bra that was more push-up-and-*out,* and those red lips were probably stopping cars a mile away. No wonder guys were craning their necks to look at her. She looked like a silver-sprayed slut.

Phoebe looked over, her gaze sliding right past Ellie.

She doesn't recognize me in my glam goth finery.

Bill wouldn't recognize her, either, not immediately anyway. If only she'd remembered to get his cell phone number, she would have called him and bypassed all this. But she didn't have his number, didn't know anyone who did, and she wasn't dumb enough to attempt a surprise visit on the set.

Tommy finished reciting the rules.

"Thanks, I'll be sure to follow them." She glanced down at the list. "How long before I'm on?"

"You're last, number sixteen, so forty-five minutes or so."

She'd spent the afternoon watching burlesque videos on YouTube, practicing the shimmy, several struts and a move called "shakin' the front porch, shakin' the back porch." She'd always done well in dance, which she'd studied in high school and college, so she had a reasonable confidence that she'd pull this off.

Static crackled over the speakers. "Testing, testing." The woman's voice had the easy, polished tone of a radio announcer. "Can everybody hear me?"

"No!"

"Turn it down!"

"Will you marry me?"

She laughed. "Lively group! We're working on some technical issues, so bear with us. Meanwhile, my name's Didi. I'll be announcing the acts, playing the music and being the bad guy who'll yank anybody or anything that's X-rated off the stage. So keep it sexy, not X-y! Other than that, I'm here to make sure you all have a good, good, good time at our Good Vibrations contest!"

People clapped and whistled.

Ellie looked around. No Bill.

"Our contest will be starting momentarily," continued Didi. "If you brought your own version of 'Good Vibrations,' please leave it with Tommy, the cute Deadhead who's managing the sign-ups. Otherwise, I'll be playing the Beach Boys' version. Contestants will be judged on ingenuity, creativity and ability to keep the beat. Couples win double points! Have fun! Contest starts in five minutes!"

AS FAR AS BILL was concerned, there were no excuses for being late, unprepared or sloppy.

Tonight he was guilty on two counts.

He strode through the festival crowds, past flashing lights, food vendors, endless barkers' enticements— "Step right up! Everybody's a winner!" He'd left the set shortly after seven, still answering questions on his cell as he walked across the beach toward the festival where he was supposed to meet Ellie at the Good Vibrations contest, hoping she hadn't given up on him.

Although maybe she had hours ago. Problem was, he was the kind of guy who didn't take the word *no* for an answer. Or *asshole* as an ending.

He heard the Beach Boys' "Good Vibrations" song before he saw the sign. Closer, he saw dozens of people milling about, laughing, drinking, some dancing.

Through a break in the crowd, he saw a couple on the stage, both dressed in red T-shirts rubbing each other's backs in time to the music with what looked like industrial-sized vibrators.

He strolled through the crowd, looking for Ellie. Walked past a guy playing "Good Vibrations" by rubbing his fingers around water-filled glasses, another practicing the tune on his harmonica. But no Ellie.

Finishing a loop around the small stage, he approached some hippie-dude sitting with the sign-up sheet.

"Has an Ellie Rockwell signed up?"

"Ellie?" He trailed his finger down the list of names. "No Ellie. Sorry, man."

"Mind if…" He took the list, started scanning. "*El Queen of Evil?*" Couldn't be anybody else.

"She's here." He bobbed his head. "Last act."

For the first time in hours, Bill smiled. "Do acts hang out in a special place?"

"No, everybody just hangs till they hear their name."

"Well, if you see her, tell her I'll be standing—" he looked around "—next to the guy with the glasses of water." Easy landmark.

"Sure, dude."

As Bill worked his way through the crowd, a woman's voice announced over the speakers, "Let's give a hand to our next contestant, Bingo Huttner and his harmonica!"

Bill positioned himself next to the guy with the water glasses, who was creating an ethereal mix of pitches by rubbing the rims.

"You're going to play 'Good Vibrations' on those?" he asked.

The man stopped, looked up. "No, I'm going to play Rachmaninoff's Piano Concerto Number Two in C minor."

Man, he sure had a knack for pissing off people today.

"Bill?"

A woman, looking like a sexy Winona Ryder in *Beetlejuice,* stood in front of him. Her voice was familiar. That spiderweb tattoo peeking over the top of her corset was even more familiar.

"Ellie," he murmured, shaking his head from side to side in rare wonder. "What have you done…"

His gaze traveled down the long fishnet gloves, the black-and-red corset that offered up two creamy mounds, the ruffly skirt bunched high like a curtain over a show of legs in black fishnet down to her…thongs?

"Bill?"

He looked up, fighting a grin.

"Are you laughing at me?"

He scratched his chin, not wanting to put his foot into it again. She'd already walked away once today. "I was amused at the fishnet and thongs, that's all."

Her deep purple lips twitched. "I'm wearing them so I can walk, silly." She held up a plastic bag. "The stilettos are in here."

A hot thrill jagged through him as he remembered her in those shoes, quickly cooling when he caught the intensity in her eyes. Anger? Disappointment? Her makeup was like a mask, making him dependent on what he interpreted in her eyes.

"I'm sorry about what happened today," he murmured. "And being late tonight. Sullivan wanted another meeting after shooting stopped, and by the time I left the set, I had no idea how late it was." He held up his wrist. "Lost my watch today."

"Bill!" squealed a female voice. A shapely flash of silver bounced to a stop in front of him. "Remember me?"

Only a man who didn't like women wouldn't have looked at her jiggling breasts, unencumbered by a bra. If he hadn't seen the line of her sleeves, he'd swear she'd been spray painted with silver.

Obviously she'd seen what caught his eye because she gave them an extra shimmy. "It's me. Phoebe."

"Right." He started to turn back to Ellie when Phoebe tugged on his arm.

"Hey!" Locking her eyes on his, she spread her red lips into a smile that had sex written all over it. "Guess what I am?" she whispered.

"Phoebe, I don't have time for this—"

"Oh," she said, turning serious, "I almost forgot that Sullivan asked me to give you a message."

He frowned. "I just talked to him fifteen, twenty minutes ago."

"Actually, it was Curtiss who called me a few minutes ago, had a message from Sullivan."

Curtiss was her boss, so it made sense he'd call her. "So, what is it?"

She leaned forward, the movement pressing a silver-sprayed breast against his arm. Those red, wet lips whispered huskily, "He said you have to guess what I am."

"What?"

She made a *brrrr* noise with her mouth. "I'm a vibrator!"

He shook her off his arm, feeling pissed at himself for falling for such a dumb come-on. That "Sullivan asked me to give you a message" line was very good, very cunning. Everybody on the set knew Bill would say "how high?" whenever Sullivan said hop.

Those red lips moved closer. "Want to be my Good Vibrations partner?"

He stepped back. "I already have a partner."

But when he turned to Ellie, she was gone.

THE QUEEN OF EVIL was royally pissed off. And hurt. And disappointed. She regretted she'd spent all those hours this afternoon practicing and preparing for this effing contest.

And she'd never have announced her intention to jump his bones if she'd known there'd be another woman's breast planted on them.

When Phoebe lured in Bill with that line about Sullivan having a message for him, Ellie decided to book. The day Sullivan needed to call a silver-sprayed vibrator to get in touch with anybody was the day Phoebe ran her own telecommunications company.

Bill was too smart to fall for that. Or too whipped by Sullivan. Either way, Ellie hadn't wanted to waste another millisecond of her time there, so she'd wandered down the midway to this quiet picnic area next to a closed concession stand. Besides a couple making out at a far table, she was alone.

Which was good because she felt as though she was going to cry.

Blinking back tears, she set the bag next to her on the seat. "Great," she muttered to herself, fishing in the plastic bag for the hand mirror. If she cried, her face would end up looking like a Rorschach test. Finding the mirror, she squinted into it at her shadowy reflection. Too dark to really see.

She tossed the mirror back into the bag, then looked up at the man in the moon. "What do you think Bill saw when he looked at me tonight? I think he didn't like the Ellie he saw."

So, it was the cliché beach babe, blond, tanned look that he desired, not the Ellie underneath. She felt a little silly reaching that conclusion since, if she were totally honest with herself, she'd known it the moment he first talked to her after the audition. After all, when he'd seen her goth that first day in the parking lot, his only interest in her had been if she'd move her car.

He doesn't accept the real me.

For a hard moment, she hated the man she'd held in her heart all these years.

"You know you don't believe that," said a male voice.

She jumped.

A man leaned against the concession stand, puffing on a pipe. Odd to see someone at the festival dressed in a businesslike white jacket and pants, although his bald head and mustache fit right in. She guessed he owned this stand, and was probably enjoying a quiet smoke at the end of the day.

You know you don't believe that? Oh. He'd obviously overheard her self-pitying whine about Bill not liking what he saw in Ellie tonight.

He strolled to a nearby table, the thick, sweet scent of pipe tobacco in his wake, and hitched his foot onto the seat. A cloud passed over the moon, and in the milky darkness he looked almost otherworldly. Like a ghost.

She shook her head, amused at her imagination. If *he* looked otherworldly, she could only imagine what she looked like.

A roar of laughter billowed from the Good Vibrations contest.

"Sounds like they're having a good time," he said.

"Hmmph."

"But you're having a bad time."

"Yeah, well, it's been one of those days."

"Want to talk about it?"

She snorted a laugh. He probably meant well, but the last thing she wanted to do was talk about her problems to a total stranger. "Thanks, but no thanks."

She gathered her bag, stood, looked around. She didn't want to walk back down the midway, which would take her right by the Good Vibrations contest. The last people she wanted to see were the breast-slinging human vibrator and what's his name.

Unfortunately, the midway was the only way.

"You wouldn't happen to know another route out of here besides the main one, would you?"

He tapped the bowl of his pipe against the table as he shook his head. "You'll have to walk through it, can't walk around it."

Like that was a lot of help. "Okay, well, thanks." She turned to leave.

"If it's worth fighting for," he said, raising his voice, "then fight the good fight."

She looked back, frowning. "What?"

"Cinderella doesn't make it home before midnight, but that's not the end of her story."

Somebody else had said those exact words...this man couldn't be...Magellan?

No, Magellan had that Jimmie Buffett clothes thing going. Plus, this man was too low-key. He'd probably been in the audience that day, then tonight overheard her whining to the man in the moon about Bill and he'd remembered Magellan's "message from the spirits" to her.

Although seemed odd he'd remember it word for word....

"I need to take off, too." He lowered his foot, looked up at the moon. Emitting a yawn, he stretched his arms. Something sparkled on his hand.

She recalled Magellan's pinkie ring, the blue sapphire.

As he started walking away, she called out after him.

"Wait!"

He paused, looked back.

"Your ring...is it sapphire?"

"Yes," he said, sounding pleased she'd noticed. "It's the stone of destiny."

The exact same words Magellan had whispered to her. No one else, not even Bill, could have heard that. As strange as it seemed, he *had* to be Magellan.

"You want to know your destiny, don't you?" he asked.

All she could do was stare, tongue-tied. She'd hoped that Magellan would say something to validate another dimension, that spirits really did whisper messages, yet she'd walked away disappointed.

But tonight, the way he'd seemed to read her thoughts, appear out of nowhere, even use the very word—*destiny*—that she'd thought about in conjunction with Bill just a few hours ago, well, this was it. She was open, ready for the mystery to be unveiled.

She nodded her head, her heart racing.

"Your destiny is...Gonzo."

Gonzo?

Had he said *Gonzo?*

The guy was a nut.

She watched him prop the pipe back in his mouth and stroll away.

She really didn't need any more of this beach-vacation time, thank you. Much saner to pack up and go home, get the coffee shop ready for the big move.

Another blast of applause and yells. She turned toward the Good Vibrations game, steeling herself for the walk past the activities, dreading what she might see. How she'd love not to be walking alone. What sweet revenge it'd be to have Bill see her in the company of some mammoth-sized hunk, his beefy arm wrapped protectively around her, his face darkly Byronic, his attitude edgy and wild like a Lou Reed.

She sighed, starting walking.

If only there really were a Gonzo.

13

MINUTES LATER, Ellie neared the Good Vibrations contest. She slowed down, eyeing the midway where it curved past the crowd of people. Unless she wanted to crawl behind game booths and trespass vendor stands, she had to walk the walk.

Maybe if she slouched, kept her eyes on the ground, she'd look smaller, less obvious.

She did so, staring down at sandy beach littered with cigarette butts, bottle caps, tossed ride tickets. Somebody jostled past, shoving up against her so hard, she nearly lost her balance.

She straightened, angry. "Hey, watch where you're going!" A few people looked back. Someone laughed. She suddenly felt pathetic, being angry at someone and not sure who.

Worse, she felt as though she'd given away her power.

Not just because some stranger had thrown her off balance, but from a lot of things these past few days. Because she'd changed her looks to please people, to get a job as an extra. Because she'd stayed that way to keep Bill interested, then switched back to test him. She'd spent so much energy worrying and being afraid if she'd be accepted, she'd lost her sense of self.

Ellie Rockwell was better than this.

She'd survived a father's desertion, parented a mother and prevailed as a businesswoman. It hadn't been easy, but she'd met the challenge each time, and in doing so learned power took many forms…from money to knowledge to sometimes simple charm. That's why she got the Queen of Evil tattoo, because she believed that character had been misunderstood. The Queen of Evil, she'd tell people, wasn't evil, she was powerful.

Cheers erupted from the contest.

Ellie adjusted her crown, smoothed a hand down her skirt. She'd faced worse in her life. Pulling back her shoulders, she headed down the walk.

The Queen of Evil was back.

"WE'RE HAVING A BIT of technical difficulty," announced the female voice over the speakers. "So we'll be taking a short break before our last contestant, El Queen of Evil."

Bill, standing at a taco truck across the midway, jerked his gaze toward the Good Vibrations contest. "Jimmie, she came back."

Jimmie stopped pouring hot sauce into his taco. "How do you know?"

He jabbed a thumb in the direction of the contest. "They just announced her act."

"El Queen of Evil?"

"Not sure why they added the El, but yes, that's her. How could you forget the tattoo?"

"Didn't *forget* it." Jimmie smiled. "I just don't memorize every detail about Ellie, but then I'm not the one who's in love with her." He took a bite of taco.

He thought Bill was in love with Ellie?

With a nervous laugh, he stood, fished in his pocket for change. "Hey, I talked your ear off because I've been frantic trying to find her. Doesn't mean—"

"That you love her?"

"Yeah, something like that," he muttered. He pulled out a wad of bills. "So, what do I owe you?"

"You know, when you talked my ear off, you talked about a lot more than just *looking* for her." He swiped a napkin across his mouth. "You talked about her eyes. Fishnet. Her shoes…"

Remembering those polka-dot wedges made Bill smile. Remembering those stilettos, on the other hand…

"I'm easing into this part, my friend, because I remember too well what it was like interviewing you for my screenplay. You didn't just hate talking about growing up in East L.A., you *detested* it. I had to pull the information out of you, like a dentist extracting a bad, but firmly entrenched, tooth. So when you run into me at a festival and want to talk, and a lot of that is about your past, I know how significant that is." He paused, studying Bill's face. "Hate to go poetic on you, but history binds hearts. Especially shared history."

"Being around Ellie these few days has brought some memories of the old neighborhood to the surface, that's all. Anyway—" he flipped through his money "—I'm married to my career. No time for love."

"That union you got going with *Sin on the Beach* needs some marriage counseling."

"If it's so great for you, why do you stay?" He laid a bill on the counter.

"It's only a paycheck while I plan for the real deal." He pointed at the bill. "Too much."

"Take it."

"How 'bout we place a bet?"

Bill smiled. "Double or nothing?"

"Sure."

"What're we betting on?"

"That you'll be joining the married men's club in the near future?"

Bill laughed. "Hate to see a good friend lose money, but if you must, you must." He looked over at Good Vibrations. "Gotta go. Give my best to Bev."

As he threaded his way through the hubbub of people, he heard Jim's booming voice behind him.

"So long, loser!"

ELLIE STOOD IN THE CENTER of the small stage, wishing the Queen of Evil still felt as cocky as she had a few minutes ago. It was one thing to storm the citadel. A whole other bag of beans to be inside it, dozens of eyes watching your every move.

At least she'd arrived during the break, which gave her a few minutes to check out the stage, quietly walk through her steps. She'd scanned the crowd a few times, hadn't seen Bill. Which made her feel weird. Bad. Confused. She recalled something Lou Reed was once quoted saying—"Life is like Sanskrit read to a pony." He was right.

Over the speakers, static crackled and hissed. "We're back, Good Vibers! Technical difficulties fixed. We hope." Laughter. "We've made a management decision. Another sound drop during this last act, and we call it a night. Performance will be judged on its partial. Then we'll tally up the scores, and announce the top three winners, which will also be posted on the contest sign."

Clapping, whistles.

"All right, everyone give a hand to our last contestant…El Queen of Evil!"

Whoops, yells.

Ellie frowned, looked at the announcer, who smiled back.

"Ready, your majesty?"

Her stomach did a slow-motion lurch. This was really happening. *Life is like Sanskrit read to a pony. Life is like…*

She nodded. Go, Team Java Mammas.

The music began, its moody, pulsing beat familiar and calming. Closing her eyes, she relaxed into the music, swaying slightly, feeling it as it built to a dark, rumbling sound. Like the ocean at night, churning its secrets from the deep.

Excitement tingled at the base of her spine. She stretched, releasing the thrill up her vertebrae, feeling its heat lick along her backbone, teasing and tonguing a path, the heat spreading until her entire body finally melted into the sound.

Music had always been her escape, her refuge. She'd lose herself in the sounds and words, gradually letting go of her world, immersing herself until her awareness was pure sensation and sound.

She was almost there now....

The contest, the people, the stage were slipping into another dimension...leaving her conscious of her body and its fluidity, how it felt to move and sway to the music...to be lost in sensation....

Suddenly, she recalled that feeling with Bill. The delicious feeling of being lost in his kiss, his touch....

A trickle of notes brought her back. She opened her eyes, resisting the urge to scan the crowd. Instead, she stared over the tops of their heads, focusing on the faintest threads of orange and pink in the dark blue sky.

The beat changed. She followed, rolling her shoulders side to side, gliding to the music. As the music trembled on a single note, she did a small, slow shimmy—she'd learned this years ago in dance, easily recalled it while practicing today—her movements building with the music, going faster, bigger.

A wolf whistle split the air.

She smiled, liking the encouragement. *See what you're missing, Bill?*

The tune shifted. She dropped the shimmy, slid out one stilettoed foot, the silver chain sparkling in the light. When the drum beat, once, she gave a little kick.

"Queenie, you kick, girl!" someone yelled.

The partying crowd was loose, fun, supportive. Sure, she wanted to win for the Java Mammas, but even more, she wanted to enjoy herself, get silly, have fun. She hadn't done something wild and crazy like this in years!

The beat picked up. For a moment, she forgot what she'd planned to do, but remembered in time to catch up with the beat. Fisting her hands on her hips, she bumped her hips as she strutted across the stage in a move called "you want it, you got it."

You know what, Bill? I have it, but you don't get it!

As the tempo thumped, she bumped her booty to the beat, coyly peeling off a fishnet glove. She was having so much fun, she barely flinched during a minor traffic jam of fishnet and fingers. Several tugs, and she was back to the beat.

Sort of.

She'd lost her place in the music again! As she listened, trying to remember, she waved the glove in the air, keeping time with the music. Some started clapping along. A few sang. She felt like a funky, sexy camp counselor leading everyone in a sing-along.

The music surged into a familiar cacophony of sounds.

Okay, she remembered this part! This is where she did that burlesque move called "shakin' the front door, shakin' the back door." Unlike shimmying, she'd had to practice this over and over. Well, here goes…

While her lower body sidestepped, her upper body shook. Shakin' the front door, baby, shakin' *it*. She nearly stumbled as she started back, but caught herself. After waiting a beat, she hunkered down and shook her back door so hard, it got a round of applause!

Eat your heart out, Bill!

She felt more zany, alive and boldly bodacious than she had in years. Before this vacation, if someone had told her she'd be digging being an exhibitionist, she'd have said they were crazy. But here she was, the center of everyone's attention, playing the tease, and she was loving every single moment of it.

Song was winding down. Realizing she still carried the peeled-off fishnet glove, she had an idea. A little naughty giveaway.

With a grand flourish, she made a show of tucking the glove inside her cleavage, leaving a little hanging out.

She looked around, pointed at a man in the audience.

He whooped, raised his fists in victory. "I won!" he yelled.

She laughed. Locking eyes with him, she strutted up to him, then leaned forward slightly, giving a little shimmy, letting him have a shot of her quivering breasts and cleavage…in her peripheral vision, she saw his hand reach…

Then jerk back.

A yell.

She looked up as a pair of brown hands reached out, grabbed her by the shoulders. Her breath grew ragged as she stared into a pair of dark, angry eyes set in a fierce face.

Bill!

"That's enough," he growled, muscles bunching along his jaw. "Stop."

His dark, territorial gaze should have struck terror into her heart, but only made it pound harder. A smart woman would defuse the situation with a joke, a quiet word, a passive gesture.

Not the Queen of Evil.

Her face hot, her heart racing, she squirmed, her mounds shimmying with the effort.

"Make me," she growled.

For a long, hot, suspended moment, he looked at her. Then he raised a dark, scornful eyebrow. "What?"

"I said—"

He slammed his mouth over hers, his hands gripping her arms, hers gripping back, their kiss hard, punishing, filled with dark energy and an intense, carnal rage that should have been terrifying.

But it thrilled her right down to the pointed tips of her stilettos.

He suddenly ripped free from the kiss. Still

gripping her arms, he stared down at her, his nostrils flaring with each sharp, inhaled breath.

Vaguely she realized she'd fisted his shirt in her hands, holding him in place in case he had other ideas. The music had stopped, even the crowd was quiet, the only sounds the faint clatter and shrieks of a distant ride and its occupants.

A burning urgency crackled between them, as though every teasing word, move, insinuation they'd made these last few days had coalesced into this scorching moment.

"I'll make you," he growled.

In a rush of movement, he leaned over and scooped her up, lifting her effortlessly. As he straightened, she experienced a giddy flashback of the Ferris wheel, the exhilarating assent, and then the stop at the top of the world where nothing else existed except the two of them.

She wrapped her arms around his neck, chills scattering over her body as she held on for the rest of this ride.

As he started walking across the stage, a thief with his treasure, the crowd starting whistling and clapping, the noise so loud it was impossible to hear whatever Didi was saying over the microphone.

Ellie leaned close to Bill's ear. "They think this is part of the act."

"Well, I was *supposed* to be part of it, if you'll recall."

As he carried her down the festival midway,

people flashed them looks, a few bewildered, some startled, most amused. It dawned on her she'd forgotten her thongs, could never manage the sand in these heels, but who cared? She'd crawl if she had to, but no way she was putting the brakes on this real-life fantasy. The queen was busy being abducted by a ravaging marauder intent on plundering and pillaging and she hoped a whole lot worse.

Jump his bones? She was going to pulverize them.

As a group of people parted, making way for them, a guy with a blond Mohawk winked at her, mouthing "give me your number."

"I'll give it to you," cut in Bill, pausing. "It's five-five-five in-your-dreams."

The guy's smile vanished, as did he.

If he hadn't, Ellie wouldn't have put it past Bill to take it a step further. Like a street fighter, he was savage, primal, and she'd be a liar if she said it didn't excite the hell out of her.

They were in front of some kind of giant Twister game, with couples bent and stretched all over each other. Outside, bright lights swirled to the old Chubby Checker "Let's Twist Again" classic.

Bill pressed a gentle kiss against her hairline, making her shudder. She looked up into his face, mesmerized by the reflection of red, blue, yellow lights playing on his brown skin. The vibrant colors reminded her of his dragon tattoo.

She hadn't given him enough credit. Anybody who chose a tattoo like that wouldn't be turned off by a glam goth chick. Made her feel a little dumb to have worried so much, to have even set up tonight's goth test to see his reaction. When the time was right, and there weren't so many distractions, she'd open up about her life and stop playing hide-and-seek.

After all, Ellie Rockwell was better than that.

Feeling relieved, she planted a return kiss on his cheek, tasting its salty wetness. Although she preferred to think his heavy breathing was solely due to sexual arousal, he'd obviously overexerted himself.

"You can put me down now," she murmured, "I'm too heavy."

"Too heavy?" He dipped his head again, so close she felt the warm puffs of his breath against her skin. "My Ellie is just right."

My Ellie? *Just right?*

Oh boy, now he'd done it.

If she wasn't so determined to impose some kind of logical boundary around her heart, or at least pretend to do so, she'd just open the portals to her heart and soul right now and admit she was and had always been desperately, unequivocally and completely head over heels in love with him.

Instead, she sank against him and let his words wash over her. *My Ellie is just right.* She looked up at the sky and its smattering of stars, took in the whirl of music and voices, the scents of cotton candy and corn dogs, mentally burning the imprint of it all into her brain. She wanted to remember it all, this moment, his words. Just as she used to document him in her girlish journals, she wanted him, tonight, forever branded in her woman's memories. She closed her eyes. *Remember, remember.*

Laughter jarred her back. She opened her eyes.

A couple, laughing, ran past, the girl squealing, "There it is! *Sin on the Beach* Freak Dance Fantasia!" Almost simultaneously, loud rocking music started blasting.

Ellie looked over Bill's shoulder at a dance floor packed with people gyrating, bumping and writhing all over each other.

And in the midst of it, a woman who could almost pass for Sara's twin, shimmying her body all the way down and back up some hunky surfer guy.

A twin wearing Sara's clothes.

The crowd shifted. Other writhing, grinding, dancing bodies blocked Ellie's view.

Wow. Ellie turned back, amazed. Hardworking, nose-to-the-grindstone Sara was getting into some serious mojo.

Time for Ellie to get some, too.

She put her lips against Bill's ear and whispered hotly, "How about you put down just-right Ellie and save that energy for something else." She trailed her lips to his earlobe and suckled, leaving no doubt what that something else might be.

"Okay," he said quickly, lowering her to the ground.

Their arms around each other, they gazed into each other's eyes, oblivious of the sounds and people around them.

"Your place or mine?" he murmured huskily.

"I'm within walking distance," she whispered, pressing her body against his. "Except, I don't know if my roommates are coming home." She thought of Sara. "Well, one definitely isn't, but the other—" did Candy and Matt's sensible sex agreement mean no sleepovers? "—could be home, and it'd be nice to have some privacy."

"I don't have roommates, so sounds like it's my place then." He kissed the tip of her nose. "But we'll have to drive to Venice."

She snuggled a little closer. "That's, what... thirty minutes?"

"Twenty if I'm not stopped for speeding."

She gave him a slow, mischievous grin. "Let's go, lead foot."

14

MINUTES LATER, they exited the festival and ran barefoot on the cool sandy beach, the lights from the festival offering visibility for another thirty or so feet. Beyond that, except for the lights of cars buzzing along Pacific Coast Highway, it was dark.

"My car's parked up there." Bill gestured toward the highway. "Down by the billboard."

Ellie, her stilettos dangling by their straps from her fingers, stopped. "What billboard?"

He hugged her with one arm, pointing with the other.

She groaned. "I thought that was a parked truck! It'll take us days to get there!"

"I know, parking sucks in Malibu. Everybody's stuck along the highway."

"Even if you're the director for *Sin on the Beach?*"

"First, I'm not the director, yet. And actually, it's no sweat finding a spot close to the set because we all arrive so early in the mornings."

She looked over. "Oh, I see…the billboard is about where the filming takes place."

"Tell you what. We'll take a short rest, then start walking. C'mere…" He pulled her closer and nuzzled his chin against the top of her head. "Ouch."

"What? Oh, the crown."

He pulled back, frowning at her head. "So *that's* what that is. I thought maybe you were picking up signals from outer space—"

"The queen is not amused!" she said with a smile, throwing her shoes over her shoulder for dramatic effect. Fumbling with the pins in her hair, she flashed on her odd encounter with the Magellan clone. "Who knows," she murmured, "maybe I have been picking up signals."

"I'll help." Tossing his flip-flops aside, he joined in, pulling on a strip of foil, but mostly enjoying the sensation of her silky hair, the warmth of her fingers brushing his.

"You're not helping," she teased.

"Yeah, but it feels good." He lifted strands, liking how they felt sifting through his fingers. "You look different with black hair."

She stilled for a moment. "Does that mean you like it?"

"Sure, it works on you."

"But do you *like* it?" She held out her hand with several pins. "Put these in your pocket for me?"

He didn't understand her sudden concern, but he'd learned long ago that when women asked about weight, hair or clothes, the smart man flew low under the radar.

"So, you'd like it if I kept it black?" She tugged

on a strip of foil. "I mean, is that an acceptable *Sin on the Beach* extra-in-the-background hair color?"

"Sure, it's acceptable. What's important is that *you* like it, Ellie."

He reached out, took the ball of foil, tossed it into a nearby trash can.

"Nice shot," she said admiringly.

"*You're* nice," he murmured, touching her cheek. She felt so warm, so soft…so there. So significant in the blur of his life. Everything had been moving so fast, he hadn't even realized how superficial it all felt, what poor company a film set could be, what poorer company he was as he ran from one task to the next, from one woman to the next, never stopping because to do so meant he'd have to confront his loneliness.

A loneliness that went away when he was with her.

"Tell you the truth, Ellie," he said, stroking her cheek, "you could have purple hair with green streaks, and I'd still like it."

They both laughed, growing quieter as their eyes met. He cradled her face, amazed at the connection he felt with her, wanting more of her. Not just her body, but her mind, her free spirit. What did she like to read? Did she like chocolate? Was she a morning or night person…

Did they have the potential to be more? Maybe Jimmie had been right…maybe Bill had fallen in love….

And she wondered if he liked her *hair?*

"Ellie," he murmured, his heart tumbling like the dark waves in the distance, "it's *you* I like."

He lowered his hands, his fingertips grazing the softness of her shoulder, the roughened texture of lace along the sides of her corset, the slickness of her satin skirt. Wrapping his hands around her, he cupped her bottom and pulled her gently against him.

"It's you I want."

He leaned down and pressed a kiss in her hair, drowning in the lavender scent of her shampoo, trailing his lips down her impossibly soft cheek.

"You," he whispered.

He brushed his mouth against hers, sharing her sweet breath.

"You," he murmured, "You…"

He pressed his mouth to hers, nibbling her plump top lip, tasting, teasing, before sliding his tongue between her lips. She opened her mouth for him, emitting a low, throaty sound of such pure pleasure, he felt himself get hard.

The feel of her nails scraping lightly on his neck stimulated him even more. He took the kiss deeper, invading the wet warmth with his tongue, seeking, exploring, wanting her so much his entire body ached.

With a low, prolonged shudder, Ellie gripped his shoulders, rising up and positioning herself until her pelvis pressed against his erection.

"Oh…" she whispered, "that's…so…good."

It was better than that. Holding her tightly against him, he looked around. A few couples were exiting the festival, cutting up to the highway.

"No one can see," she murmured, thrusting against him with small, controlled movements.

"Ellie…"

"Shh…oh yes, stay like that." She thrust lightly again. "They'll just think we're kissing…."

She looked up into the shadow of his face, moaning as his lips found hers.

Insinuating his body closer, feeling her flattened breasts against his chest, he groaned as their kiss picked up where they'd left off, their tongues coiling and curling and sucking, her pelvis making him crazy with those small, tight thrusts.

Cupping her bottom, he crushed her against his swollen need, growing even hotter thinking about that short, teasing front panel of her skirt. It wouldn't take much to lift it all the way and slip inside….

He yanked back his head, breaking off the kiss.

She looked at him with a stunned expression, her mouth open, those luscious mounds quivering with each breath.

"What?" she whispered shakily.

He glanced toward the billboard as he swiped a hand across his slick brow. "Okay," he said, turning back. "Now that we've rested—"

"You call that *resting?*"

"You know what I mean." He mindlessly flapped the edge of his shirt, as though that might cool him down.

"Oh, no!" she said, shaking her head vehemently. "I'm not taking a two-mile hike after *that!*"

"Ellie." He rasped a laugh. "It's not two miles—"

"I'm not through resting!" With a grin, she fisted her hands on her hips to stand her ground, teetering slightly.

He sputtered a laugh. "Okay, I get your point. I'd like a nice big rest, too, but it's time to go."

"No."

"We can't stay here."

"No?"

"No." A couple walked past, laughing, waving good-night. He nodded, waved. "See what I mean?"

"They're at least forty feet away!"

"For crissake, Ellie, you want to do it right here, in front of everyone?" He blinked at the why-not look on her face. "My God," he murmured, "you really are an exhibitionist!"

She rolled her eyes. "And this from the man who stormed the stage like King Kong."

"Like you didn't love it."

"I did," she whispered. "Every single moment."

The way she looked at him gave his heart a squeeze.

"But to go back to your question, no, I don't want to do it where people can see... I mean, that's great fantasy material, just not so hot in the real world."

"You—" He blinked. "You've done that?"

"No!" She paused. "Have you?"

"No!"

She studied his face for a moment. "Three-way?"

He cleared his throat. "Let's grab our shoes, hit the road."

She gasped. "More than once?"

"I can't believe we're—" He blew out an exasperated breath. "Once. Okay, where'd you toss your shoes?"

"*Only* once?"

"Only once."

She made a vague gesture toward the south. "Me, never. I was invited to, but I really didn't like the guy. His girlfriend was nice, but..." She scrunched her face. "Not my thing."

"Thanks for sharing," he muttered, checking the sand.

She looked out toward the black, distant waves. "Although I wouldn't want to do it where people could see, I wouldn't mind if it were darker...."

"Well, it's not darker, and your shoes aren't over here."

"Here's one..." She halted, looked over at him. "Never mind, false alarm." She picked up his thong. If he had to keep looking for it, they'd have to stay here longer....

She loved how the light played on his body. Wearing so few clothes—shorts and a shirt—there was a lot of naked to see on the man. When he crossed between her and highway lights, she caught jagged flashes of his silhouette. The outline of a muscled leg. The curve of a bicep. Even the dark, threadlike shape of his fingers.

She recalled the different ways those fingers had touched her. Feathering lightly across her back. Burrowing into her hair. Or, just moments ago, crushing her greedily against his swollen groin.

Her sex throbbed. She was so hot, so turned on....

"I'll look over here," she called out, sauntering toward the beach, looking at him over her shoulder. When his back was turned, she smiled, tossed the thong aside. It'd take a long time to find it, if it was even findable in the dark.

In a matter of steps, she'd crossed into the dusky night, where she tugged loose the satin ribbon that threaded together the front of her corset. Standing near the shoreline, she paused, listened to the distant pounding surf. A low-flying plane, its light blinking, seemed to coast in front of the moon.

She pulled apart the top of the bodice, sucking in a sharp breath at the onslaught of cool air against exposed skin. She wanted to make it as easy as possible for him to do the things she wanted to do. Fumbling in the dark with the ribbons and buttons on her corset was the last thing she wanted them to be spending their time on.

"Found one of your shoes," he called out.

She strangled back a laugh. This guy needed to be reeled in, get his priorities straight. If she wanted to go hunting for shoes, she'd go on a shopping spree with her girlfriends. Right now, all that mattered was to be together in the dark, immersing themselves with each other, feeding their hunger.

She strolled toward him, feeling bold, sexual, a predator stalking its prey. Unashamed, primed, ready to indulge her needs in the moment…not later, but here, now.

As she approached, he halted his search and straightened, watching her, a question in his eyes.

"Ellie?"

He stood on the edge of the light, not bright enough for him to see she'd loosened her top, or recognize the look in her eyes. But even a blind man in the dark could feel and hear….

She stopped inches from him, her breasts rising and falling with her needy breaths. She took his hand and pulled it to her, laid it gently on her pushed-up, swollen breast.

"Oh, yes," she said, her control growing ragged as chills rippled through her. "I love your hands on me," she whispered. "When you touch me, it's unbelievable how it makes me feel. It turns me on, makes me ache for more."

Even in this hazy light, she saw a hot, needy look flicker to life in his dark eyes.

She leaned forward and lightly touched her lips to his.

Once.

Then she pulled back and, ever so lightly, trailed his hand down over her loosened corset, letting him feel how it barely contained her spilling breasts.

"I'm so horny," she murmured, "I could probably come with a single touch."

Then she gently released his hand, turned and started walking toward the shoreline, not bothering to look back because she knew he'd follow, ready to do her bidding.

The queen had spoken.

FEW THINGS threw Bill off. He was like a bull in that way. Solid, grounded, fearless. But wave a red flag, and he'd snort and bellow and paw the ground, intent and focused on one thing and one thing only.

That is, after he regained his motor skills. For the moment, it was all he could do to remain standing. The breathy ache in her voice, the creamy plumpness of her breasts, the knowledge that she'd loosened that sexy corset had left him foggy, disoriented…and incredibly turned on.

He dropped the shoes and followed.

Stumbling across the sand, he kept his eyes on the wavering mirage of her pale back and arms. The rest of her, the black corset, black skirt, black hair, seemed to merge with the night.

The sand softened under his feet, moist from the recent tide. He paused, let his eyes adjust to the darkness. In the distance, waves sparkled under the moonlight. Somewhere out there, the noise of distant surfboards chopping and cutting the waves sounded almost like a hand stroking skin.

"Over here," whispered Ellie.

He turned, momentarily awestruck at the sight.

She looked otherworldly, a vision in black, her face hovering and faint. Like a siren in the velvet night.

Not enough light to distinguish features, but enough to grasp shapes and movements; he realized she held out her hand. She seemed so comfortable here. He smiled to himself. Perhaps because this was her realm. Yes, indeed.

The Queen of Evil.

He grasped her hand, pulled her into his arms. Lowering his head, he felt dizzy with the feel, the scent, the warmth of her. Just holding her made him crazy for relief. He gritted his teeth, fighting the need even as it spiraled higher, hotter. Burrowing his lips into her silky hair, he inhaled its rich scent like a man taking his last breath.

"Lavender," he murmured, an image flashing in his mind. Summer. Fragrant purple blossoms. "I remember now," he whispered, warming to the memory, "your mom was always watering lavender bushes along the side of your house."

"You remember the funniest things."

"It's all in the details," he murmured, burrowing a hand into the silky mass. "Lavender is like you. Vibrant and sweet."

She laughed softly. "I'm not that sweet."

"That's right." He nuzzled the sensitive patch of skin behind her ear. "Not when you're the Queen of Evil."

His hands hungrily roamed over her back, sliding over an expanse of satin, like liquid under his fingers.

"When I first saw you tonight—" he slid his hand up her back, luxuriating in the silky warmth of her skin "—your breasts pushed up like that, your legs exposed underneath that naughty skirt—" he released a ragged breath "—I thought I'd died and gone to heaven."

He slowly stroked his flattened palm along the back, up, then down.

"It opens in front," she murmured.

"Thanks for the directions," he whispered, capturing her earlobe with his teeth. He nibbled and suckled, excited by her small moan of pleasure.

She suddenly grabbed his head and pulled him into a deep kiss, teasing her tongue into his mouth with a low, needy moan that shot a blast of heat right down to his groin. She slid her tongue in and out, licking and sucking, her frenzy building.

Ellie suddenly jerked back her head, her lips leaving his with an audible pop. She stepped back, just out of reach.

He took a deep breath, confused. "You okay?"

She half laughed, the sound light, teasing. "Very okay." A moment passed. "Can you see what I'm doing?"

He blinked, straining to discern the pale movement of her hands in the dark. "No."

"Listen."

He heard a wisp of satin. A succession of light snaps.

"I'm taking off my corset."

The black peeled off, dropped. In the moonlight,

he saw her naked from the waist up, the tips of her breasts dusty against her soft, pale skin. Her lack of inhibition driving his need higher.

"Touch me," she whispered.

He closed the space between them, gently, gently reaching for her breasts, stifling a moan as his palms brushed up against her soft, full mounds.

"Yes." She shuddered.

She pressed against him, filling his hands, her nipples nestled against his palms. He brushed them lightly back and forth, back and forth, his need flaring higher as he felt the tips swell and harden, heard her whimpers and moans.

He invoked the memory of her baring her breast when they'd stopped at the top of the Ferris wheel, the jolting thrill of seeing its pebble pink tip, the creamy sheen of her mounds. "Later," he murmured, "I want to see you naked under the light... all of you..."

As she groaned her agreement, he squeezed and kneaded her breasts, then tugged and rolled her hardened nibs, watching her pale body arch with pleasure.

He lowered his head, taking one taut nib into his mouth, flicking and sucking it while stroking the lush weight of the other. When she cried out, he increased his torment, sucking and nipping the sweet puckered nipple until she lay in his arms, her back arched, her head tossed back, her breasts thrust forward as she whimpered she wanted more...more....

"Ellie," he whispered, lifting his head slightly, "you're driving me crazy."

With a needy sound, she gripped his head, holding it in place. He looked up at her pale face, the swirl of night and stars behind her head, imagining her a wanton pagan, a mysterious goddess, a demanding queen. Tightening her grip on his head, she slid and rubbed one nipple, then the other, against his lips, murmuring dark wishes which he greedily obeyed.

And then he was kissing her again, forcing her head back, his lips driving into hers, nipping, devouring, his need furious and hot and urgent...ready to spread her, take her....

Ellie leaned back, momentarily stunned at the beast that had risen in Bill's place, his mouth demanding, his tongue aggressive, his words explicit and coarse. She'd never been kissed this way, kisses that intoxicated and tormented, made her entire body ache and throb for more.

A beach babe would hate it.

This goth chick loved it.

This powerful, commanding, potent man's needs were like a searing stake to her heart, killing off all pretenses while igniting in her a lusty, unrepentant creature whose desires would not be denied. A snarl, guttural and disturbing, rolled up her throat, the primal sound lost in his ravaging mouth.

An instant later he ripped his lips away. Turning her around, panting, she faced the dark, glistening ocean. He nestled behind her, whispering into her ear.

"You hot little exhibitionist," he murmured, taking a moment to suckle her earlobe before continuing. "Let's pretend you're on stage, the wild elements your audience...."

As he spoke, he trailed one hand down to a breast, circling her aching nipple.

"Lift your skirt," he murmured, his lips moving against her neck, making her skin prickle.

She did, and he slid his fingers inside the elastic band of her fishnet stockings, inside her panties, gently separating her folds, his touch feather soft, seeking...

"Tell me where," he whispered, nuzzling her cheek.

She opened her mouth, tasted the salty air, his ministrations on her breast igniting a line of liquid heat down to her groin, where his other hand deftly, lightly circled her nub, waiting for her command.

"A little to the left," she murmured, gasping as he found the spot.

"Is that good?"

She tensed, clutching the skirt as passion whipped through her blood. "Yes," she gasped, the word dissolving into a moan as his fingers worked their magic. His lips nuzzled her neck as he dipped one finger, then two into the slick crevice.

"You're so wet," he murmured huskily.

Shuddering in her throat, she tilted her pelvis forward, rising eagerly with his building tempo.

Through slitted eyes, she looked out at the dark churning ocean, its cool breezes rushing over her, causing her skin to prickle pleasurably. She felt deliciously decadent, unabashedly wanton. Never in her life had she indulged her sexuality like this, felt safe enough, trusted enough to let her fantasy go.

She spread her legs wider to experience more sensation, her hips grinding involuntarily with the expert movements of his fingers. Her body was oh, so hot, on edge, shaking and quivering as he slipped and slid between her legs, harder and faster, driving her higher....

"Come for me," he growled.

The creature released a prolonged, needy groan.

"Yes, sweetheart," he murmured. "Give it to me, let me hear you, feel you...."

Her body shivered all over, the sensations building inside her until she didn't think she could take any more. Her entire being on edge, ready to burst, so hot, so ready.

Suddenly, release ripped through her, ecstasy so exquisite, so savage. She threw back her head and cried out, sinking against Bill's hold, riding and rubbing his hand, again and again, until the spasms gradually lessened....

She sank against him, heaving breaths, sated and sleepy, vaguely aware of his arms wrapped tightly around her waist, his chin resting on her shoulder.

They stayed that way for a quiet moment, looking out at the endless black ocean, the sparkle of moonlight, the scatter of stars.

"That's the best I've ever had," she finally whispered.

"Think so?"

"Know so."

He gently turned her around, reached into his pocket and pulled out a small square packet, held it up for her to see. "Brought it to work because I knew we had this date...."

"Even after our, uh, episode on the set, you still brought it to the Good Vibrations contest?"

"Never say never."

She smiled, taking it from him. "Me, too."

"That's what you were thinking, too?"

"Not thinking, *saying.* I made a vow this afternoon to jump your bones."

He choked back a laugh. "Before or after our, uh, misunderstanding?"

"After."

"If I'd known you were that confident, I wouldn't have worried."

"Not confident." She ripped open the packet. "Determined."

He sucked in a sharp breath as he felt her touch him, gingerly, on the outside of his shorts with her free hand. He grew instantly harder, his urgency rising like a tidal wave. "I've been so horny, so worked up," he whispered, spreading his hand around the back of her head, pulling her closer, "I could probably come with a single touch."

She laughed low in her throat, the sound incredibly seductive. "You're stealing my line."

He leaned his forehead against hers, strangling

back a groan as she caressed him. "I'd like to steal you," he murmured hoarsely. "Steal you away, keep you with me forever."

When she pulled down his shorts, he emitted a sharp hiss, biting back his need as she gently rolled the condom over his aching, swollen member.

Then she stood back, quickly removed her fishnet stockings and undies.

"Oh, yes," he whispered, tugging her to him, roaming his hands over her naked bottom, back, massaging and squeezing her breasts, finally taking her arms and wrapping them around his neck.

"Hold on," he whispered. When she did, he lifted one of her legs, hooking it around his hips.

She clung to him, teetering on her one standing leg. "I don't know if I can—"

"Just lean into me. I'm strong."

"You can say that again," she said, followed with a lusty sigh as she found her balance.

He wedged his erection up hard against her cleft, stroking it against her wet, slick opening, then rubbing it against her apex, around and around, teasing and tormenting her hot, sweet little clit.

"Right there," she suddenly gasped. "Oh, yes… there…"

She dug her nails into his shoulder, the sharp stings spiking his arousal even higher.

"Take it easy," he murmured, half meaning it. Her released inhibitions excited him, made him want her more than ever. He pressed his hips forward, while guiding himself into her stretched opening, filling her slowly, slowly.

He lowered his mouth to hers, took her deep into a hard, rough kiss. Whatever subtlety, whatever lingering finesse he'd pretended to have, shattered to pieces. He tore his mouth from hers, breathing hard, grinding his teeth as he sank into her, holding her arching body. As he seated himself fully within her, she released a deep, guttural groan.

"You...feel...so...good," he moaned.

He lightly rocked his hips, keeping his movements short, controlled, syncing his rhythm with hers. She clung to him, whimpering, begging for more. He gave it to her, thrusting as hard and deep as the position allowed him, her gasps of pleasure taking him higher, hotter, her pulsing hips pulling him in.

Need pounded through him, merging with the sounds of the distant thundering waves. He wanted to devour, ravage, plunder her sweet, ripe mouth, her hot skin...his need so hot, so raw. He spread his legs, leveraging himself as he stroked deeper, harder....

Her body tightened, tensed, then with a shriek she clawed at the air, her insides clamping down around him, squeezing, milking, driving him to that glorious point of no return....

In a mindless fever, he clutched her body tight against his, giving one last thrust.

His breath exploded as he cried out her name,

clutching her as release exploded through him, again and again, to a mind-jarring satisfaction.

For a long moment, they simply held each other, their spent bodies moist with exertion, their heaving breaths mimicking the rhythmic tumbling of the ocean.

Finally, she dropped her leg, laid her head on his chest. Bill ran his fingers up and down the bumps in her spine while she fiddled lazy fingers at the nape of his neck. Balmy breezes lifted strands of damp hair, offered cooling respite to their skin.

"Wow," Ellie finally murmured.

"You can say that again."

"So…" She pulled back, looked up into his face. "How far is it to that billboard again?"

"Not far," he murmured. He kissed the tip of her nose. "As long as we resist the urge for more rest stops."

15

FORTY MINUTES LATER, they walked into Bill's Venice apartment, located on the third floor of an old brick building on Ocean Front Walk, the famous paved beach path that ran the length of Venice Beach. The windows were open, filling the place with the scent of the ocean. The distant sounds of laughter and bongo drums could be heard from the ever-present partiers along the walk.

She looked around his perfectly ordered room, which looked more like an office than a home. Against the far wall sat a metal desk and its swivel chair, bracketed by a bookcase and a large metal file cabinet. Over the scarred wooden floor lay a faded rug, its corners at precise angles to the walls. A black leather couch sat opposite an entertainment center that looked like a guy's dream world—oversize TV, video game player, an XM radio setup.

On the clean white walls were some framed certificates, a few film posters. No photos.

Bill stood in front of the entertainment center. "What would you like to hear?"

"Got Lou?"

"Lou Reed, eh? That's right, you like his music. The former glam rocker, current rock and roller, right?"

"Close enough." She was pleased he didn't sound critical. He'd taken what she'd said to heart the other day.

He picked up the XM radio. "But you have to admit, that guy's had more styles than a Macy's department store window. Let's see what we can find."

"Lots of people go through different styles. Look at Madonna." She wandered over to one of the film posters. The background was a man's face in blue, in the foreground was a dancing woman. Frederico Fellini and *La Dolce Vita* were in big yellow letters. "Do you like Italian films?"

"Not Italian films as a genre. More I like Fellini for his inventive filmmaking."

"*La Dolce Vita.* That means—"

"The Sweet Life."

"Remember how they used to call the hood *la vida loca*—the crazy life? Now with all the new businesses and money moving in, people are calling it *la dolce vita.*"

"That'll be the day," he muttered. "Hey, can't find anything Reed-like. If you don't mind groovy beach music, how about Jack Johnson?"

"Sure." She crossed to his bookcase, checked out his collection of books on film, a shelf of bounded scripts, a slew of Kellerman, Hiaasen, Patterson novels. Funny to think of him directing a *Baywatch* clone when his tastes ran to more complex stories and characters.

The moody surf tones of Jack Johnson started playing. A song about a guy wanting to make love to his girl.

Bill's arms wrapped around her from behind, his body swaying in time to the beat. He hummed along with the tune.

She leaned against his warmth, her concerns fluttering away. Being with Bill, listening to sexy, sultry music was definitely *la dolce vita.*

"If I don't eat something soon, I might collapse before we get to the good part." He straightened, turned her around. "Like pastrami?"

"Pastrami." She gave a breathless little laugh, struggling with the quick switch from hot to mild. "I like. Yes."

"Good. Remember when I told you I make the best sandwiches this side of New York? Now I'm going to prove it to you. You can wash up while I get it ready."

"Wash up?" She touched her hand to her face, realizing what their heated beach interlude must have done to her makeup. "Please tell me I don't look like a Rorschach test."

He chuckled. "Bathroom's down the hall. There's cleanser in my medicine cabinet, hand towels underneath the sink. Dinner, my sexy lady, will be served in bed."

Moments later, she stared at herself in the mirror, groaning at the black smudges around her eyes, the smeared red on her mouth, the mottled white on her face. Fortunately, it'd been dark all the way from the beach to his building, so he'd only had a few minutes to see her like this.

She found the cleanser, wondered if it was Vi's, but so what? If she'd found other girlfriendlike stuff it would have felt weird, but the bathroom was all male—no extra toothbrush, no makeup, no tampons.

Smearing the cream over her face, thinking of all the other times she'd spent hours putting makeup on and taking it off, for the first time she wondered if she really wanted to keep doing this. Not that she wanted to stop cold turkey being a glam goth, but maybe like Lou Reed, she could shift a little, ease up on her style, on her life, on herself....

She swiped the towel across her forehead, down her cheek, her glowing tan-in-a-can skin showing through. She was starting to feel like an archaeologist, digging through the layers of Ellie. What was underneath the glam goth makeup, the fake tan, even below the pale skin, was, she realized, a mystery even to her.

SETTING THE PASTRAMI, mustard, pickles on the counter, Bill doubted she did things like this for herself. After a day of making coffee and serving food, he imagined her collapsing into a chair with a nuked meal, listening to...Lou Reed? He shook his

head, smiling. Marilyn Manson, Siouxsie Sioux, Lou
Reed. Other women were often too predictable, too
cookie-cutter. They worked out at the same places, ate
the same things, shopped for the same clothes. Eventually, predictability led to boredom and he bailed.

Unlike Ellie, who had a habit of shaking up his
world, keeping him on his toes. He liked that.

Layering the meat on a slice of bread, spreading
the mustard on another slice, evening it out just so,
he thought she needed somebody to do this for her.
Maybe she surprised him, but he surprised himself
even more realizing he wanted to be that somebody.
As he selected the best pickle in the jar for her
because only the best would do, he finally admitted
to himself how deeply his feelings for her went.

It seemed funny to have these epiphanies while
making a sandwich, but on the other hand, he took
great pride and care in making sandwiches. Not so
odd that other things he cared deeply about would
float to the surface.

He remembered a bag of chocolates he kept in the
back of the cabinet. He set one, wrapped in shiny gold
foil, on the edge of the plate. It stood out, nearly perfect,
bringing that special extra touch to the ordinary.

Carrying the plates to the bedroom, he realized he
would love Ellie Rockwell until he drew his last breath.

"DINNER'S SERVED!" he called out, rounding the
corner into his bedroom. He stopped cold, his breath
halting in his throat.

Ellie, naked head to toe, smiled shyly. "Hi." She looked at the plate. "That's an awesome-looking sandwich."

He looked her over, from her dark glossy hair, over her heart-shaped face, lingering a moment on her lush, pear-shaped breasts, quickly dropping over her tummy to a final stop on the curling hair at the dark apex between her thighs.

"I have legs, too," she whispered teasingly.

He ducked his head with a laugh, feeling like a schoolboy caught with mirrors on his shoes, as he scanned her legs.

"Very nice legs," he agreed. Looking back at her face, he murmured, "All in all, you're awesome-looking, too."

She laughed, pleased.

He set the plate down on his dresser. "I've suddenly lost my appetite. For food anyway."

As he approached, that simmering look in his eyes leaving no doubt what was coming next, she felt her nipples tighten as a sweet, liquid heat permeated her body.

"I thought you said if you didn't eat first," she whispered teasingly, "that you'd collapse."

"I did." He stopped right in front of her, his gaze melting into hers. "And I will."

Ellie gasped with delight as he dropped out of sight, collapsing to his knees in front of her.

He cupped his hands around her bottom, and tugged her to his mouth. Gently opening her folds, he inhaled deeply, emitting an animal sound of pure pleasure at the scent.

"You smell so sweet," he moaned, planting kisses on her mound, flicking teasing licks along her opening. He nudged her legs farther apart, his pulsating tongue slipping inside, a man on a mission, going after exactly what he wanted.

"Oh, yes!" She grabbed onto his head, teetering slightly as he delved deeper, stroking and licking. His lips were a marvel as they lapped at her tight knot, made her crazy, on fire, her hips and thighs quivering with the exquisite torment.

Just when she didn't think she could take more, he delved a thumb into her wet core, settling it masterfully alongside his relentless tongue.

The combination was like a torch to jet fuel, shooting her heat and moans sky-high.

Keeping his thumb going, he looked up at her, an unholy grin on his face. "I love seeing you like this," he murmured.

"Good," she gasped, pushing his head back into place.

The vibrations of his muffled laughter only added more exquisite sensation to his wickedly talented tongue and thumb, making her delirious with need, her body shaking like a missile on a launch pad, ready to blast off any moment. "Oh yes…right there…"

She suddenly sucked in a breath, holding it as her entire body froze, suspended, on edge….

Tears stung her eyes as the first orgasm rocked her, hard and fierce and swift, the sensations crowding each other, one hitting before another ended. She clutched his hair, back, shoulders, her body undulating, pulsing.

His thumb working her, he looked up. "Want another?"

"Are…you…crazy?" She blinked, looked down. "Yes!"

He drove her pleasure on, giving her another climax…and another…until, exhausted and spent, she grasped his hand and pulled it away, her core still spasming from his touch.

He kissed her tummy, her breasts, her cheek, then nuzzled her neck as he held her quivering body.

"Wow," she murmured, "that's the best I've ever had."

A throaty chuckle. "That's what you said the last time."

"Yeah, but this time I really mean it."

He led her to the bed, helped her lie down.

"We'll see about that," he said, positioning himself over her.

AN HOUR LATER, they sat up in bed, naked, munching on the sandwiches.

Ellie wiped her mouth, picked up a pickle. "This is the best sandwich I've ever eaten."

He nearly choked as he swallowed. "Ellie, c'mon, the best sex…but also the best sandwich? You're going to give me a big head."

She snapped a bite of pickle, giving him a lecherous look. "Speaking of which, I'd like to do that next...."

He held up his hands in a sign of surrender. "Rain check, okay? This man needs his sleep before the alarm goes off in—" he looked at the clock and groaned "—five hours."

"What time is it?"

"Midnight."

They looked at each other.

"So," he said, wiping his mouth with a paper napkin. "Is the carriage turning into a pumpkin?"

She looked intently into his eyes. "I'd almost forgotten about that. No, it's not. But maybe Cinderella's dress is turning into sackcloth."

He frowned. "What?"

She thought this would be easy. Especially after his softening on the topics of Marilyn Manson and Lou Reed, he didn't seem judgmental about how people looked. Because that's all that her confession was about, right? How she liked to dress and wear makeup differently, like the way she had tonight...no big deal, really.

But her throat had tightened, and her nerves felt hopelessly tangled. Because this was more than how she looked. On a deeper, visceral level that she didn't completely understand, she needed to know Bill accepted her no matter what she looked like.

"I'm not who I've been pretending to be."

He set down his sandwich. "You're married."

She rolled her eyes, fighting the urge to laugh. "No. As I told you, there's nobody else." She took a breath, released it. "Remember a few days ago, before the festival opened, you were at the beach trying to get a Benz moved?"

A funny look crossed his face. "Yes, but how did you know that?"

"I was the goth chick reading the *Sin on the Beach* festival poster."

He stared at her.

"You called out to me. Asked if that was my Benz."

Awareness dawned. He blinked, feigned a double take. "The spiky black hair?"

She nodded.

He looked at her black hair, which fell softly about her face. "No wonder you asked if I'd like your hair to stay black. You were…testing me."

An edge had crept into his voice. "Bill, I'm really not a manipulator, if that's what you're thinking. Yes, I tested you, but…can you cut me some slack here? Maybe I liked that you liked what you saw, and I didn't want…to lose you."

God, she felt pathetic. She felt like the twelve-year-old Ellie again, idealistic and dreamy and angst-ridden over Bill Romero, who could squash her world with just a look.

I'm better than that, dammit.

Outside on Ocean Front Walk, somebody whooped, followed by a clanging sound like a bell.

Bill glanced at the window. "That's Venice Beach for you, never a dull moment."

"Yeah, it is, isn't it?" she said sarcastically. She picked at a spot on the bedspread. "Look, as silly as it might sound, I've been freaked out ever since we got together about admitting my goth self to you, and after my confession tonight, I would have appreciated the respect of a Bill Romero truthful answer, like 'I hate glam goths so get out of my life,' or 'glam goths are better than French women' or even 'I don't care let's go to bed.'"

He grabbed her arm. "Whoa, Ellie, let's not make this bigger than it is."

She met his gaze dead-on. "Then if it isn't bigger than it is, what is it?"

He shoved aside their plates and drew her into his arms. "I want to laugh, but I'm afraid you'll take it the wrong way. The truth is, I work in a business where people look different every day. And of the women I've dated, some have changed their styles so often, they make you look like a stick in the mud."

"Like Vi?"

"Vi, yes, she changes her style. Not such a surprise as she runs a clothing shop."

Clothing shop. As though the sexually charged, overly perfect French woman wasn't perfect enough, she now had a business that rivaled Ellie's fledging clothes-design business.

"So, after this week, can I visit you at Dark Gothic Roast, see you in your element?"

Visits? Is that what their future held? She clutched at the bedspread, needing something to hold on to, forcing herself to stay cool, composed. "Sure, come visit."

"You said it's moving soon? To here?"

"Plan is to move into a storefront near Boyle Heights."

"East L.A.?" he said, incredulous. "Ellie, why in God's name would you want to return there?"

She was starting to feel as though she were on an emotional roller coaster. One moment she was tied up in knots making the big confession that she thought would be a fireworks display, but instead sizzled and sputtered into nothing but smoke.

Now she was suddenly embroiled in the topic of her upcoming business move, a discussion that for her was harmless, boring even, but it had suddenly exploded in her face.

"You sound angry," she said, surprised.

He exhaled sharply. "I don't know if *angry* is the word. Astounded, perhaps."

"Critical?"

"Critical, you bet your ass! Moving back to the hood is just plain dumb. Gangs aside, you're a businesswoman, or so you've told me, and you want to move into a region where nearly thirty percent live below the poverty level? Where the hell do you expect to get customers to buy your products?"

With a sickening jolt, she realized this issue, not the one of her looks, was the lack of acceptance she'd been so fearful about. His jaw was tight with tension, his eyes were cold with disbelief and anger.

It's none of his business, she told herself. But as soon as she thought that, her insides caved in because deep down, she'd hoped the two of them would return to their community, their roots, together.

"I don't want to explain my reasons," she said quietly, collecting the plates to give herself something to do. "I already told you and Jimmie the reasons why. Suffice to say, the neighborhood is changing for the better, and I want to be part of that change. Mom's going to be the bookkeeper for my business, hopefully for the others I rent to, as well. It's an opportunity for her, too, because she'll own stock in the business, be a part of something that's growing."

He nodded, a smirk on his face. "You should talk to Jimmie about renting some of that space for his indie company."

"The company he wants to partner with you?"

"An independent film company is a small dream, Ellie, with small returns. Just like your moving back to the hood is a small dream, Ellie, with even smaller returns. I dream big. That's the difference between you and me."

She felt raw and exposed, resentful and hurt. The plan she'd been nurturing for months—frightened but excited at the venture of expanding not only the coffee business, but other ventures—had just been unilaterally trashed.

She slid off the bed, picked up the plates. "I'll, uh, take these back into the kitchen. It's late, and you have to get up early, so why don't you get into bed."

As she left, she remembered Magellan's words that day she and Bill had been on the stage—*Cinderella didn't make it home before midnight, but the story didn't end there.*

Boy, did he have that wrong. Cinderella didn't make it home before midnight, but she should have because the story didn't just end, it had just come to a grinding halt.

AT SIX THE NEXT MORNING, Ellie slipped inside the beach house, trying not to make any sound so as not to wake anyone.

"El, is that you?" Candy, dressed in a white bikini bottom, a white shirt tied around her waist, did a double take at her hair. "You dyed it black again?"

Ellie nodded, shutting the front door behind her.

"Wearing your burlesque skirt with a *Sin on the Beach* T-shirt?"

"Yeah, it's the new goth beach look. Part Sandra Dee, part Elvira."

Candy laughed, then gave her friend a saucy look. "So if you're sneaking in, that must mean…"

Ellie wandered into the kitchen to make coffee. "Bill and I had a date, yes."

"You sound a little—"

"Just tired, that's all." She didn't want to talk about it. Not yet. As she filled the coffeepot, she glanced at Candy. "And unless you've started sleeping in your bikini bottoms, I think you just sneaked in, too."

Candy blushed. "Yeah, but it's not serious, of course. Just—"

"I know. Sensible sex." Maybe she should have tried that plan with Bill. Made a lot more sense than her midnight one, that's for sure. "How's our Sara? Did she sneak in, too?"

"Not yet." Candy sat at the kitchen counter, grinning like a kid. "Pretty good vacation, eh?"

"Sure is." Ellie busied herself pouring coffee into the filter, getting down the mugs.

"I have a business luncheon today. Do you have another call on the set?"

She did, but she didn't want to go. "Yes."

"Cool. I bet Bill drools every time he sees you in one of your killer bikinis."

"Yeah," she said softly, thinking how he was anything but drooling when he'd dropped her off. This morning they'd been pleasant to each other. Quite civil, actually, in an aren't-we-being-grown-up-despite-our-devastating-tiff kind of way.

But it had sucked all the same.

He'd given her a quick kiss on the lips goodbye, she'd said something casually cheery like "Have a great day," but her move to East L.A. had definitely built a cold wall between them.

"Well," Candy said, heading off, "gotta hit the shower, get ready for the luncheon. It's so cool you and

Bill got together after all these years. I swear, El, it's like one of those Disney movies, where despite seemingly insurmountable obstacles, true love wins out."

"Yeah," Ellie muttered, "a real Cinderella story."

She flipped on the coffeemaker, not sure whether to laugh or cry.

16

ELLIE WASN'T SURE if she was a sucker for a challenge, a fool for an insurmountable obstacle or if she had too much time on her hands. But here she was, eight hours later on the set, playing a semigoth, sorta-glam beach babe extra. Which meant she'd spent the day sashaying around in a string bikini that barely covered her goth tats, fluffing her dyed-black-over-blond hair and slathering sunblock on her fake tan.

Peter, the happy-go-lucky assistant casting director made a twirling motion, which she'd come to recognize as a time-out signal.

"Okay, people," Peter said, the lighted cigarette in his hand weaving smoke into the air every time he gestured, "take fifteen. And I don't want anyone—" he pretended to look over all of them, but let his gaze linger on Ellie so she'd get the message "—fraternizing with any of the crew, including the director. Understood?"

He'd made this speech every break, as though, given the opportunity, Ellie would break loose from the pack like some kind of rabid beachnik and make a beeline for Bill as she had yesterday.

Which she'd never do, of course.

It was bad enough she'd shown up for work.

The carriage had turned to a pumpkin, the horses to mice, but Cinderella obviously had a stubborn streak, because she'd returned to the ball minus the magic.

Ellie wandered over to a cluster of chairs and umbrellas—the extras' break area—and sank onto a white plastic chair, shielding her eyes as she looked out at the ocean, that vast blue entity that had witnessed her and Bill's heated lovemaking last night on its shore. It saddened her to realize it would never happen again.

"Hey, Ellie, what's up?" asked Gus, sitting in the chair next to her. He stretched out his long tanned legs. He wore his customary red board shorts, but today his T-shirt read Surf Shack, which Peter had fretted about and quibbled over before the shoot, citing some contract fine print about extras not wearing logos other than ones for the show's sponsors, but giving in after Gus eloquently argued that the Surf Shack, being a real Malibu hot spot, gave the show a touch of authenticity.

"Doing okay," she lied.

"Me, too." He pulled a comb out of his pocket and raked it through his white hair. "Tell you the truth, I was surprised you showed up on the set today after that little brouhaha yesterday."

The *little brouhaha* being the tension between her

and Bill when she'd been one pestering body too many at the director's station. Funny to think there was that brouhaha, then last night's brouhaha... Was the problem that she and Bill were just too passionate to be together?

Nah. Passion was one of the better things about their being together. More and more, she was realizing their problems were, oddly enough, cultural. When most people had that problem it was because of different cultures. Their problem was their common one. He hated East L.A.; she dug it. His whole thing was about overcoming his past, hers was about returning to it.

"We got over that brouhaha," she said casually. But would they ever get over the culture issue? She didn't think so.

"Outside," murmured Gus, a surfer term referring to large waves building far from shore. He slipped the comb back into his pocket. "Looks like a gnarly wave headed straight for Bill."

She looked over. Sure enough, Sullivan, his face pinched, was marching across the sand toward Bill. The group hovering around him instantly scattered.

Blasts of Sullivan's words could be heard all through the set.

"Why the hell did you?...I don't care!... I told you no and you did it anyway!"

Bill's voice was low, the words unintelligible.

"Don't care!" Sullivan boomed. "And furthermore, you're fired!"

Ellie clutched the arms of her chair, watching as the two men stared each other down. She held her breath, expecting the next sound to be fists smacking.

But Sullivan abruptly turned and marched back to his trailer.

"This job meant everything to him," she whispered.

"Not that I don't feel sorry for the guy, but maybe that's part of his problem," Gus said.

An eerie silence descended over the set, the only sounds the creaking of a boom mike and the distant crashing waves.

After a moment, Bill ripped off his headset, snatched up his notebook, and without even a glance at the crew or the actors, walked away.

Ellie stood, her heart pounding, imagining his devastation. Despite what had happened between them, her heart reached out. He'd told her how, starting with film school, he'd spent years honing his skills and working toward a job such as this one where he'd finally have the opportunity to prove himself as a director.

And now that opportunity had been torn away from him.

She disagreed with his need to dream so big, but she wasn't so small as to abandon a friend.

"Tell Peter I'm leaving," she said to Gus.

"You coming back?"

"Nope." She started walking after Bill. "My beach babe days are over."

BILL HEARD Ellie's urgent pleadings behind him, but he kept walking. He didn't want to talk to anybody, deal with anything. His throat scalded with the words he'd held back, the accusations he'd wanted to scream at Sullivan. The guy was a *line* producer, not a creative producer. Which meant he was the bean counter, the budget-meister, the money cop who watched the bottom line and never had anything, *anything,* to do with the artistic aspects.

Unfortunately, the invisible executive producer had given Sullivan free rein to be whatever he wanted to be.

Bill cursed, pissed at the entire film industry that broke people's souls, pissed at Sullivan who'd micromanaged the shoot to failure, but mostly pissed with himself because he'd gambled his career on this gig and lost.

"Bill, please wait!"

"No, Ellie!"

"C'mon, I'm your friend." A short yelp. "Ow, ow, ow!"

Blowing out an exasperated breath, he turned, glowering at her. Ellie, black hair flopping in her eyes, was jogging in place, her face tight with pain.

"What the hell—" He looked down at her bare feet, his frown deepening. "What is it with you and shoes? Either you're wearing heels too high, wedgies too unmanageable or you're barefoot on hot sand. Are you crazy?"

She winced, blinking back the pain. "Probably,

but that's beside the point. I was worried about you. Didn't want you to go."

He saw the twelve-year-old girl again, who'd run out barefoot in the middle of the night, desperate to know if it was really true, was he leaving....

Shaking his head, he walked back to her. "C'mon," he said, opening his arms, "I'll carry you."

"No! That's not why I followed. I wanted to be here for you, not—"

He lifted her into his arms, shifting her weight to get comfortable, then turned and continued walking, this time more slowly, across the sand. Sunbathers looked up. A guy with a boogie board cut in front of them, grinning.

"Bill, please, put me down."

"No."

"You're under enough stress, you don't need to be carrying me."

"Yeah, well, you don't need to be searing the skin off the bottom of your feet, either." He blew a drip of sweat off his lip, tightening his grip on her.

He walked in a straight line across the beach as though he had a purpose, as though he knew his goal. But in truth he was lost, more lost than he'd ever been. But he kept moving forward because it's all he knew to do, aware only of the hot sun on his skin, the salt in the air, the feel of Ellie in his arms.

Ellie.

He tightened his hold on her, holding her closer, needing her as he never had before.

"Ellie," he whispered, his voice fractured, "I'm nothing."

"No!" She cradled his face with her hand. "You lost an opportunity, but you didn't lose yourself."

He snorted a laugh. "You don't understand Hollywood. Newbie director gets fired from first gig? It's like a death sentence. Nobody will hire me now. Nobody."

A couple of kids, carrying bright plastic buckets and shovels, screamed and laughed as they waddled in front of their parents toward the shore.

"Maybe," she said, treading carefully, "this is a sign for you and Jimmie to start your company."

He walked a few moments in silence. "Never did like Sullivan. The man has an ego the size of Manhattan."

If Sullivan's ego was Manhattan, thought Ellie, Bill's was Texas.

That's when it hit her. This wasn't just about losing a job, an opportunity. It was about being big, which to Bill was synonymous with success. Directing a big film, being an A-list Hollywood power player, being a big name...because anything less— such as running an indie company—was too small to be significant.

As sad as she was for him, she was suddenly irritated, too. The kind of irritation that comes from caring and having your hands tied behind your back. She'd thought earlier how Bill was driven to overcome his past. At some point he'd decided, unconsciously or not, that he couldn't do that unless he was bigger, better than the next guy.

No wonder he felt like nothing. In his mind, he'd lost all his power.

MINUTES LATER, they reached the entrance to the festival. Bill, flushed and breathing hard, set her down on a shady patch of sand underneath an awning. "Let's go in. I'm parched, need something to drink." He looked at her feet. "And we need to get you some thongs."

"Thanks."

Catching his breath, his gaze traveled up her legs, lingering on the snug bit of material between her legs, his problems pushed aside enough to remember her taste, her cries of pleasure, the way her body trembled just before she came.

"Look," he said, meeting her eyes, "about this morning…"

She shrugged. "It's okay."

"It's just that…where we grew up…"

She quietly nodded, took his hand. "Bill, I think I understand more than you know. Let's get that cold drink."

THEY MADE A PACT to avoid reality.

For as long as they were inside the festival, they were not allowed to discuss or worry about Sullivan or *Sin on the Beach*. Comments about goths or anything gothic were fine as long as a certain someone didn't start obsessing whether she was acceptable as one. To ensure they didn't stumble into a tension-fraught conversation, neither was allowed to say the words "director" or "East L.A."

That settled, fifteen minutes later they meandered down the midway sipping their drinks, Ellie in a pair of new black thongs, two people who for all appearances didn't have a care in the world.

Suddenly Bill halted, tugging her to his side. "Ellie, look!"

He pointed to the three screens outside the Hot Shot Photo Contest, each displaying photos that randomly changed every few minutes.

Ellie nearly choked on her drink. "Oh, no."

Bill grinned. "Oh, *yes*."

Ellie's face filled one of the screens, looking shy but obviously excited. Or maybe she just remembered how excited she'd been.

"Please tell me you only downloaded the G-rated photos," she murmured.

"I only downloaded G-rated, promise. This is great. They're showing all the downloaded entries until the winners are announced at the end of the festival."

He stood behind her, his arms encircling hers. The way he cradled her, she felt incredibly close to him.

"I remember that ride so well," he said in a low voice. "The sweet scent of your skin, our first kiss... You tasted like lemonade and sunshine."

The photo dissolved as another one displayed.

"Wow!" She stared at the crisscross of her fishnet cover-up transposed over the lines of the spiderweb. "Bill, you're a good photographer!"

"That's because…"

She knew the rest of it without his saying. Because of his training as a director.

"Because I'm visual," he finally said.

"More than visual," she said gently, "you're talented, too. Look how others are stopping to look at the photo."

He nuzzled the soft pink shell of her ear, then nibbled on the lobe. "Maybe that's because of the beautiful woman in the picture."

When a close-up of a dragon head flashed on another screen, the gathering crowd oohed and ahed.

"You're a good photographer, too," he whispered into her ear.

Gasping softly, she reached up and stroked his face while continuing to watch the photos of themselves.

"It's exciting to watch us," he murmured, trailing his fingers around her waist. "We're good together, Ellie."

She held her breath, as though to release it might release the magic of what he'd said. Silly, and yet when she finally exhaled, she did it slowly, as though testing the magic of his words.

Nothing changed. He still cradled her from behind, they still stared at the photos although theirs were no longer flashing on the screens.

We're good together, Ellie.

So what if they'd had a few bumps in the road, they kept coming back together, kept reconnecting, kept digging deeper and finding new meaning in their relationship. Yes, relationship. She knew as certainly as her heart was beating that this would go on.

Maybe for the long haul?

They were at a point in their lives where they were both starting new careers. Hers with the expanded coffee shop, clothing-design business, not to mention overseeing other commercial rental spaces. His with whatever he wanted to pursue next. Starting out together, they could give each other a lot of support and encouragement, be each other's cheering sections.

Of course, he'd refuse to move to East L.A., would probably refuse to even visit her there. Which meant the commuting would be up to her, which would be stressful and difficult. A normal twenty-minute drive on the 405 could take up to three hours during peak times. No way she could handle hours-long commutes and kick off several businesses, which meant this whole damn thing was doomed before it got off the ground so why even care?

"All that stands between fear and outcome is courage, my friends, courage!"

"Hear that?" Bill chuckled. "Sounds like our friend Magellan is nearby."

"He's a nut."

"So we all are, I say." Bill pulled her around, kissed her on the tip of her nose. "The guy's funny, and laughter is the best medicine, so I say let's join the audience and enjoy ourselves."

She gave in, wanting to shake her thoughts. Bill was right. Laughter was a good thing.

A few minutes later, they stood in the crowd, watching Magellan lure a young couple onto the stage.

"Come, come," Magellan said to the guy and girl heading up the stairs to the stage. "I have no tricks up my sleeves, just the insights of my mind into your lives, and the mysteries I will foretell!"

"Do you think he'd bald underneath that turban?" asked Ellie.

"Bald?" asked Bill. "Could be. That turban fits pretty snugly."

Magellan suddenly stopped talking. Turning to the audience, he scanned the crowd.

"Ah," he said, his gaze falling on Bill, "have you learned what has roots nobody sees, is taller than trees?"

The first lines of the riddle. Bill smiled, shook his head.

Magellan nodded knowingly, his gaze drifting to Ellie. He gave her a wink before turning back to his act. "Everyone," he said, sweeping his hand to the young couple on stage, "give these brave people a hand."

Someone touched Ellie's shoulder and she jumped.

17

ELLIE GASPED, jerked her head around.

"Sis!"

"Matt!" She looked him up and down. "Wow, look at you! Brad Pitt, step aside."

Her brother actually blushed. "I'm a made-over man, what can I say?" He nodded to Bill. "We meet again, neighbor."

"How's it goin', Matt?"

"Great. Hey, El, I just saw the Queen of Evil's name posted outside the contest area as one of the winners for the Good Vibrations contest. Congratulations!"

"Cool!" Ellie gave Bill a high five.

"So, why aren't you two on the set? I didn't know Hollywood directors got to play hooky."

"Yeah, they do," chimed in Ellie. "It's one of the perks. So how's Candy? Wasn't today some kind of important business luncheon?" If she kept talking about Candy, the conversation wouldn't return to Bill's directing career. "Yes, it was. She told me this morning. Duh. I should've remembered that. That Candy, wow, is she a marketing powerhouse or what?"

Matt started to speak.

Ellie cut him off. "She deserves recognition for that, too. Which will happen of course when she gets that team leader thing at SyncUp."

"What?" asked Matt.

"You know, that team leader position—"

"Candy *knew* about that?"

"Sure! That's Candy for you. A mover and shaker, her finger always on the pulse of what's happening."

"I, uh, need to go." Matt started to leave, stopped, turned back. "Good seeing you again, Bill."

"Same here, Matt."

With a halfhearted salute, her brother disappeared into the crowd.

"He seems to have a lot on his mind," said Bill.

"Don't we all."

Bill gave her an approving look. "So the Queen of Evil is a winner, eh? Let's go check that out, see how she, I mean you, did."

She smiled. "I've been pretty silly...."

"Silly's good. Worrying's bad." He put his arm around her as they started walking toward the Good Vibrations stage. "Would've been nice if you'd let me in on your internal angst so I could have put your mind to rest."

"I'm not always so good about speaking up."

"Coulda fooled me."

She laughed, playfully punched him. "Bill Romero, you should know better than to mess with the Queen of Evil!"

A FEW MINUTES LATER, they stood in front of the Good Vibrations stage, now empty, where it had all happened the night before.

"Here it is!" Bill leaned closer to the sign. "Queen of Evil, you came in second place."

"Second?" She peered up at the sign. "Who knocked the queen out of first place?"

"Keep in mind, queenie, it was a tough competition. Ready to hear?"

She nodded, liking how they were playing with each other.

"First place went to...Danny Gerash and his singing water glasses."

She feigned disappointment. "If only I'd brought more water into my act."

"Obviously, that was the key." They shared a smile. "But they gave you, I mean us, *couple* points, queenie!"

"Team Java Mammas will be proud."

They stood, their arms around each other as they looked out at the empty stage.

"I have good memories of that," whispered Ellie.

"Me, too. After I got over my jealousy."

She gave him a squeeze. "The Queen of Evil got you that worked up, huh?"

"No," he breathed, stroking his hand along her arm, "Ellie Rockwell got me that worked up." He slid his hand down to hers, lacing their fingers, his warm fingers lazily stroking and rubbing hers.

"Come on," Bill said, leading her toward the stage, "I want to be a couple again."

They left their drinks on the edge of the small stage, then walked to the center where he gathered her into his arms, swaying slightly to an unheard tune.

She linked her hands together around his neck, laid her head on his chest, heady with his scent, his strength, the sweetness of the moment. The festival receded like the waves, pulling far back to the sea, leaving the two of them here in their own private world.

His hands moved down her back, settling momentarily on her hips where he pressed her against him, showing her how she made him feel. Then he skimmed his fingers back up, feathering lightly across her bare skin, up to the sensitive area of her neck.

She shuddered, looked up into his face, saw in his eyes that he hid nothing from her. Neither the pain of his dismissal...nor the intensity of his desire. He was a strong man, probably the strongest she'd ever known, which made his willingness to let down his guard and be vulnerable all the more precious to her.

He was showing her that he trusted her.

He slipped his fingers up her neck, cupping her head with his hold, his other hand gliding up her rib cage, up to the swell of her breast which he gently massaged, his body turned so it shielded his movements from others.

He leaned close, his stubble rough against her

cheek. "I want you," he murmured, his mouth nibbling seductively at hers. "I need you."

Fire leaped in her belly as he pulled her tightly against him, his hard male body against hers. Over his shoulder, she saw the curtained-off changing area still standing, hidden behind some stacked chairs and equipment. The sight was dangerous, made her think of things she shouldn't be thinking, not in broad daylight....

Another part of her said *screw it*. This man needed her, she needed him, and after what they'd been through, maybe this was all they had. Now. Here.

Not wanting to think or question, she took his hand and led him off the stage.

Moments later, after peering outside to ensure no one had seen their escape, she slid the curtain closed.

Sunlight filtered through the blue material that fluttered with the ocean breezes, the rippling light creating an underwater effect.

She looked at him, her heart hammering, her breaths suddenly shaky. All the tension, passion, heat of the day welled up inside her, burning off every last coherent thought. All she wanted was to touch him, feel him, taste him.

He slid down her bikini bottom, inched his hand into her wet curls, zeroing in on her core. Stifling a cry, she fumbled with his shorts, managed to pull them down far enough to free his stiff cock.

"No," he growled, working her harder, "you first."

She sputtered a contradiction that ended in a hiss

as she widened her thighs, her sex throbbing with his probing, circling fingers, her hand mindlessly squeezing his sex, her mouth blindly streaking his face, his lips, finally latching onto that bushy little soul patch, suckling as though her very life depended on it. A hot, bold quickie. She'd never done this before, but then, no man had ever been Bill. With him, she felt unabashedly wild, exquisitely free, incorrigibly wanton.

Panting, rubbing, licking, she suddenly rose onto her toes and arched her back, foggily realizing those depraved, needy grunts were hers.

She clutched his shirt for balance, clenching her teeth as the first climax hit, stifling her panting squeals as she rode his hand, thrusting her hips hard and tight, over and over to completion until, with a final whimper, she settled back onto her feet. Lazily opening her eyes, she pulled out his hand and, while holding his gaze, lightly flicked her tongue over the tips of his fingers.

His eyes glinted with heat and surprise.

With a wicked grin, she sank to her knees onto the sandy floor.

She took him into her mouth, his shaft so smooth and hard, his taste salty, musky. Still throbbing from her own orgasm, she groaned as she drew him into her mouth, loving his deep shudder of pleasure.

Sea breezes swept underneath the curtains, stroking and cooling her heated flesh. Cradling his balls with one hand, she juggled them softly as she twirled her tongue around the hardened ridge, a teaser before taking him in with a long, wet suck.

Tightening her lips, she pulled her mouth back up his rigid sex, stroking in tandem with her hand, repeating the movement slowly back down, up, down....

His hands tangled in her hair as his hips twitched. "Look at me," he whispered hoarsely, "Ellie, please…"

She held his dark gaze as she licked and stroked and sucked, her hands working with her tongue, her eyes telling him everything she'd never said in words.

"Ellie…" He blinked, his voice racked with emotion. "Ellie, I…"

As his release came, she took him in, coddling him with her mouth and hands, savoring his pleasure, knowing that what'd they done had been more, much more than a hot quickie. Hot and quick, yes, but they'd also made love.

Love.

Which he'd known, too, even though that was the word he'd left unsaid.

SOON AFTER, they continued their stroll down the midway, sipping their melted-down lemonades, occasionally sharing a secret smile.

If there was ever a moment in her life that felt perfect, this was it. The swirl of ocean air, the happy energy of the festivalgoers, the quiet, unspoken connection between her and Bill. For a crazy moment, she felt as though she didn't deserve this, that maybe their pact to stave off reality meant this was a dream and nothing more, that it would end after they passed through the festival gates and returned to the real world.

A cell phone rang.

"Not mine because I left it at the set," Ellie said with a shrug. "Plus I have the Lou Reed ringtone."

"How could I forget," teased Bill, flicking her an amused look as he fished in his shorts' pocket. He retrieved his phone, answered it.

"Bill here."

He listened, his face growing tight, angry. He looked at Ellie, mouthed "Sullivan."

Sullivan.

She felt an ugly foreboding, wondered if the producer was blaming Bill for more problems, maybe threatening legal action. What a mess. So much for their escape from reality.

Then, a look of surprise came over Bill's face. He glanced at Ellie, his eyes sparkling.

"No need to," he said into the phone. "Okay, go ahead… Yes… All right… Fine… Thanks, bye." He flipped it shut, dropped it back into his pocket, then flashed her a big, guess-what grin.

She returned the smile, but inside she felt chilled, afraid.

"Sullivan apologized. Asked me to come back as director."

Down the midway, the merry-go-round started, the calliope playing a lighthearted, airy children's tune. In the distance, Magellan called out for people to be brave, to have courage.

"That's great," she said cautiously, "if that's what you want."

He sputtered a laugh. "Are you kidding? Of course I want it! But that's not the best part. He's asked me to be the next director. No more tryouts, no more filling in. I'm number one, Ellie!"

He pulled her into a bear hug, squeezing her so hard, she could scarcely breathe. "That's great," she heard herself saying in a voice she didn't recognize, "just great."

He pulled back, his smile fading as he caught the look in her eyes.

"What is it?"

She swallowed, wondering if she should say what was weighing on her heart. But if she didn't, she was no better than the Ellie who'd stuffed down the truth about herself, imagining it to be worse than it really was. Maybe that was true here, too. What she imagined wasn't as bad as she thought.

"Bill," she said softly, "you're not happy in that job."

"Says who?"

Now that she'd said it, she realized her words were dead-on right. He'd have the job, the title, but he'd lose his self-respect.

"Me. Sullivan won't change. Like you said, he's a line producer trying to take artistic control. You'll live under his thumb, under his public humiliations day after day. You're better than that job."

"Better?" One black eyebrow shot up. "Look, Sullivan's an asshole, I'll grant you that. But sometimes that's what it takes to run a big, successful project." He half smiled, made a dismissive gesture. "Forget all that. The fact is, it's the kind of big break I've spent my entire career going after, and if it means I have to deal with an asshole on a daily basis, so be it."

The calliope sounded so loud, the organ music jarring. She touched her fingers to her brow, trying to shut out the chaos of people and noises around them. She lowered her hand, suddenly feeling tired and drained from the intensity of the day. "I just think you'd be happier at the independent film company—"

Bill tried to bite back the expletive, but it shot out anyway. "Sorry," he muttered, raking his hand through his hair. "You and I have a bad habit of having these arguments in the middle of the damn midway."

She twisted her mouth. "Maybe we should have made a pact about not doing that, too."

They stared each other down for a long moment.

"I think our problem," he said quietly, "is that you dream small, Ellie, and I dream big."

"*Our* problem?" She laughed. "I think *your* problem is you're so caught up in being a big man with a big career you've lost all perspective."

People were gawking, craning their necks as they walked by.

"Ellie, just because you're settling for a small dream doesn't mean I have to."

He saw the hurt in her eyes, and hated himself for

putting it there. It was inevitable, he now realized, that they'd reach this point. He could never go back, and she could never not.

"By *small*," she said, "you mean the hood."

He nodded.

"Have you ever thought that no matter how big you think you are," she murmured, "your prejudice will always make you small? You're ashamed of your roots, and until that changes, you'll be ashamed of yourself."

His face turned hard, dangerous, as his gaze delved into hers. "Let me get this straight. Just because you're going back, it's going to get better? Like, all those poor kids who think being successful is growing up to be a drug dealer and driving a Range Rover...*you're* gonna change that?"

"You're changing the subject."

"You brought up the hood, sister. Seems you think throwin' lattes at the homies will cover up all the neighborhood's problems." He held up a strand of her hair. "Let's see...this is black over blond over black...but I recall you had penny-colored hair that matched your freckles when you were a little girl. Where'd they go? In my book, people cover up the things they're ashamed of."

If he'd stuck a knife into her, it would've hurt less than his slicing words. Maybe because what he said resonated deeply within her.

The way he looked right now—his tough-guy body language, the pitch of his shoulder, the way he'd flung out his hand behind his back—brought back memories of the boy from years ago. His back up, watching out for his family. Tougher than the next guy. Not taking it off nobody.

"Doesn't take a genius," she said softly, "to figure out that someone who slathers on makeup and clothes might be covering up something, even from themselves. What's sad is the person who thinks the glitzy job, the big bucks, the fancy title disguises who he really is—a punk kid on a street corner, angry at the world for the burden and hurt it placed on his shoulders."

She watched him walk away, barely aware she'd dropped her drink, its cold liquid pooling around her feet.

In the distance, Magellan cajoled his audience. "I have no tricks up my sleeves, just the insights of my mind into your lives, and the mysteries I will foretell!"

She'd been conned by the festival and its smoke and mirrors, by the carnies and their tricks, even by the games and their promises.

But most of all, she'd been conned by love. Everything she'd felt and believed and desired had been nothing but an illusion. Had been nothing but a trick of light in her heart.

18

THE NEXT MORNING, after Ellie had helped convince
a disheartened Sara not to give up on Drew and helped
a mortified Candy recover from yet another of her
festival escapades, Ellie lied to both her pals and said
she was spending the day being an extra on the set.

Then, after they'd left the beach house, Ellie
returned to pack up and leave.

Gus, bless his heart, had dropped off her purse, so
she didn't have to go back to the set to pick it up.
After she got her things together, she'd leave a note
that there was a crisis at Dark Gothic Roast and leave.

Inside, she headed to her room, started tossing her
stuff into her bag. Holding up her burlesque skirt, she
smiled at its wet, bedraggled appearance—the result
of that lusty night at the beach with Bill—before
tossing it into the trash can.

What happened in Malibu could sure as hell
stay in Malibu.

Cinderella was finally leaving the ball. A bit
worse for wear, but that's what happened when you
overstayed your welcome.

She headed into the bathroom to wash her face. Looking into the mirror, she heard Bill's words—*In my book, people cover up the things they're ashamed of.* Was that it? She was ashamed?

Of what?

She'd certainly put a lot of time and effort into covering up parts of herself. She'd dyed her hair so much, even she couldn't remember its natural color. Her tan face was part fake, part natural, but give her a few goth minutes and it'd be artificially snow-white again.

She squinted, leaned forward. Well, surprise, surprise. There were a few freckles over the bridge of her nose, just like when she was a kid.

Made her think of her dad...he'd touch her freckles, giving each one a name...silly names, always different...Tina, Teeny, Itty, Bitty....

When he'd left, she'd blamed herself. Didn't matter if her teacher, her mother, even Matt said no, that's not the case, she did. If only she'd been better, nicer, sweeter, she'd have been more acceptable and he wouldn't have left.

She opened the medicine cabinet and collected her pancake makeup, the blood-red lipsticks, the dark pencil sticks...and tossed them into the trash. She could always buy more, but for the time being, she had the urge to let those freckles get some fresh air again.

Heading back to her bedroom, she heard someone knocking at the door. Maybe one of the girls had forgotten their keys. Or Matt had heard about the guy

Candy had dragged home last night. Well, Ellie wasn't going to give him her sisterly matchmaking caretaking advice. No, not this girl. She'd tell him that any guy who agreed to something called *sensible sex* needed to look up the word *oxymoron* in the dictionary.

She opened the door, ready to say just that, and froze.

Bill, looking sheepish and too handsome for his own good, leaned against the doorjamb. She wrapped her arms around herself as though that could contain the breathless emotion that clutched at her heart.

"Hi," he murmured. When he dipped his head, sun glinted off a gold earring.

"Hi."

He glanced at her nose, smiled. "I see your freckles."

She shrugged, checked out the smooth planes of his cheeks and jaw. "I see you shaved."

"Kept the soul patch, though." He tickled it with his finger.

"Good," she whispered, remembering it all too well.

"May I come in?"

She hesitated, dreading the inevitable sorry-let's-be-friends talk. "Shouldn't you be on the set?" she said oh-so-nonchalantly, stepping back to let him inside.

"I was."

"You're on a break?"

"Sort of."

"Well, glad things are working out." So cavalier, so together, as though her heart was still in one piece. Really, Ellie should win an Academy Award. "I'm packing, getting ready to go home."

"Oh, I'd hoped— Well, I brought good news."

"*Sin on the Beach* has a plotline?"

He flashed her an amused look. She'd miss that look.

"No." He pulled an envelope from his pocket. "We won a Hot Shot prize. Not one of the *top* prizes, but a fun one nevertheless—the Dishonorable Mention award." He handed the envelope to her.

She opened it, read the coupon for a free weekend at a five-star hotel, including meals. "Guess it pays to be dishonorable," she said a little too lightly, handing it back.

He held up his hands. "No, it's yours."

"I'd feel a little silly going alone. Maybe you and Vi?"

"You know," he said, growing serious, "that Dishonorable Mention award made me think of things in my life that were so intolerable, they'd become dishonorable. So I made a few calls this morning to fix that. First one was to Vi. Told her we're not going to have that talk."

Vi the *Kama Sutra* Wonder with the French accent was no more? Before Ellie gave in to the cheap thrill of success, she reminded herself she and Bill were no more, either.

"Made another call after that," he continued, his

brown eyes solemn. "Remember how Magellan said the bridge between fear and outcome is courage? I called Sullivan, told him I was staying only out of fear and quit. He wanted me to elaborate, so I told him sometimes big isn't better. I'm sure he'll be pondering that for days."

She let the words sink in. "You *quit?*"

He nodded. "Made another call right after that to Jimmie, asked if he'd still like me as a partner in JimBill Productions."

"I thought it was—" She smiled. "After what you put him through, he should get top billing."

"That's what I thought. He's already pulling his script from consideration at another studio—I told you he wrote that protagonist based on my life growing up?"

"I recall hearing something about that."

"Yeah…character's name is Gonzo."

For a moment she couldn't breathe.

Bill stepped closer, a worried look on his face. "Ellie, you okay?"

"Yes, I think…I need to sit down."

He followed her to the couch, sat next to her. "You're shaking."

She waved off his worry. "I'm okay, it's… Magellan."

"What about him?"

She dropped her hand back into her lap, realizing she'd finally had her first real supernatural experience. "He's the real deal," she whispered.

"You think?"

She nodded. "I know he is. It's just…I learned something too late."

Taking a deep breath, she rolled back her shoulders. "I was next on your list of things to fix, so let's get it over with."

"Over with?" Bill knew he'd been a jerk yesterday, but he'd hoped this would turn out differently. That's what he got for being a cocky, temperamental, bullheaded man. He believed his own stories, especially the ones he made up in his mind.

"Speaking of intolerable and dishonorable," he said solemnly, "I'm sorry for the things I said yesterday. You were right when you said I was ashamed of my roots, and until that changes, I'll be ashamed of myself."

This was harder than he thought, but he had to say it. "You know, it wasn't me who was the golden boy of my family. It was Reggie. He was smarter, kinder, better than all of us put together. I was busy with my studies in New York when Mom called to say he'd fallen in with a gang. She wanted me to come home, talk sense into him, but I was too caught up in myself." His voice dropped. "Sometimes in life, it's not what you do, but what you don't do."

He suddenly felt as though the facade he'd held together all these years cracked, and the loss, the overwhelming loss rose to the surface, seeped through the breaks, wiping out the years of control, but not the guilt…the horrible guilt….

"Oh, Bill," Ellie murmured, wrapping her arms around him, holding him tightly against her. "It wasn't your fault."

He laid his cheek against hers, giving in to her softness. Neither spoke for a long moment.

"I've been thinking about that riddle," he finally murmured. "What has roots nobody sees, is taller than trees, its virtues it sows, and yet never grows?"

She shook her head. "I don't know the answer."

He pulled back and looked into her eyes. "Yes, Ellie, you do. You always have. The answer is home. Roots. I want to return there, do the right thing in honor of my kid brother. You set up your coffee shop and clothing designs, Jim and I will set up our indie company. And let's make a place other than the streets for kids like Reggie."

She nodded, blinked. "Sure."

He sat up, a funny smile on his face. "Me, a guy who loves details, and I forgot the most important part." Cradling her face with his hands, he let out a long, slow breath as he looked into her bright, questioning eyes.

"I love you, Ellie Rockwell. I think I've loved you ever since that night years ago, when you asked if I was going away. I should have known then no matter where I traveled or what I did, the place I belonged was there, with you."

"Seventeen."

"What?"

She looped her arms around his neck and smiled. "That night was seventeen years ago."

He quirked a smile. "You have a good memory."

"It's not just my memory." She leaned closer, whispering against his lips. "I know because in my heart, I've loved you every single day, hour and minute of those seventeen years, Bill Romero."

And Cinderella, no longer worried about curfews or hair color or even the misunderstood Queen of Evil, kissed her prince.

Swoop, swoop, rock, rock.

* * * * *

Don't miss the conclusion to the
SEX ON THE BEACH *mini-series!*
Look for Wild Child *by Cindi Myers, coming*
August 2008 from Mills & Boon® Blaze®.

*Cool drinks, warm sand and sexy guys!
Everything a girl needs for the perfect holiday.*

Wild Child *by Cindi Myers*

*Sara Montgomery needs this vacation in the
biggest way. But getting unplugged from the mobile
phone and laptop is proving tricky. Luckily for her,
Drew Jamison arrives as the perfect distraction…*

Turn the page for a sneak preview of
Wild Child *by Cindi Myers*

The sensational conclusion to the
SEX ON THE BEACH *mini-series available
from Mills & Boon® Blaze® in August 2008.*

Wild Child

by

Cindi Myers

THE COOL firmness of sand between her toes, the smell of salt and suntan oil, the thunder of waves and the shrill cries of seagulls transported Sara to her girlhood. Walking alongside Drew, she felt that same sense of possibility to the afternoon—that wonderful anticipation she'd come to Malibu to rediscover. With a surfboard tucked under one arm, he even *looked* like the idols of her youth. Anything could happen as long as the sun shone and her companion kept smiling at her.

She glanced at him and he winked. Now she *really* felt like a girl again; it was all she could do not to giggle. She was glad she'd agreed to come with him. He was easy to be with, and he'd given her the perfect excuse to get away, though her phone was in the beach bag she'd grabbed to bring along.

Whether she could go through with her original plan to seduce this hottie was debatable. Her seduction skills were definitely rusty.

Ellie would probably say that was all the more reason for her to practice.

They passed a carnival laid out on the sand—

Ferris wheel, arcade games, a stage and volleyball nets. A man in a lime-green turban and a Hawaiian shirt stood at a booth near a sign that read Magellan the All-Knowing. "What's all this?" Sara asked.

"It's all part of the big *Sin on the Beach* party." Drew raised one eyebrow. "I figured that was what brought you here this week."

She shrugged. "My friends said something about it, but I never realized it was so…elaborate."

He nodded. "They're hosting a week-long bash—games, dancing, contests, prizes. It's bigger than spring break."

A week-long bash? "Guess we lucked out." She grinned at him. Talk about the perfect setting for a wild fling.

"My shop is just a little ways up the beach," Drew said. "My grandparents started it almost forty years ago."

"It's hard to imagine having a grandfather who surfs," she said. "It seems like such a hip, young thing to do." Her own mother—like her father before he'd died—was a serious, hard-working person. Even after they'd moved to L.A., her mom had never acclimated to the west-coast lifestyle. She complained that the sun shone too much.

"Grandpa Gus definitely isn't an old fogey," Drew said. "If anything, he acts too young. He forgets he can't do everything he could as a young man and it gets him into trouble."

"And you worry about him," she said.

He gave her a sharp look. "Does it show that much?"

"Not really. But I can relate. I'm the same way with my Uncle Spence. He's younger than your grandfather, but he works so hard. He never lets himself relax, and he worries about everything. He depends on me a lot to help with his business and I hate to let him down."

Drew nodded. "I love Grandpa, and I don't really mind, but sometimes…" His voice trailed away.

"Yeah, sometimes." She knew exactly how Drew felt. Could it be she wasn't the only young adult in the world with too many responsibilities and too much guilt?

"Would you like to see the shop?" Drew asked. "Then maybe we could do something together."

She could think of any number of things she would like to do with him—some of which involved wearing no clothes. Obviously her libido was taking the idea of a no-holds-barred vacation seriously. But even the more sensible part of her liked the idea of getting to know this man better. "That would be great," she said.

Like a bad-tempered chaperone determined to cramp her style, her phone started vibrating, rattling against the keys in the bottom of her bag.

"What is that?" Drew asked.

"Nothing." She groped in her bag, trying to locate the off button for the phone, but only succeeded in getting the strap wrapped around her sunglasses case.

"Seriously, what's that buzzing noise?" Drew moved closer. "Do you have something in there?"

"No, really, it's fine." If she broke off yet another conversation with him to take a call, he was going to think she was a complete workaholic.

He stepped back, grinning. "I've heard about those things, but I never knew a woman who carried one with her to the beach."

"It's not... You don't think—" Her face probably came close to matching the color of her swimsuit. She jerked the cell out of her bag. "It's a phone!"

He laughed. "Hey, did I say it wasn't?" He shook his head. "Go ahead and answer it. Maybe it's your roommate again."

She should be so lucky. She checked the caller ID. "No, it's my uncle."

"Then you'd better answer it."

"Yeah, guess I'd better." She flipped open the phone as she moved a few steps away.

"Sara, why haven't you called the title company?" With those words, Uncle Spence made her magical mood vanish.

The title company! She groaned. "I'm sorry. I got busy and it slipped my mind. I'll call in the morning."

"You need to call now. Granger's been asking me about the closing." She pictured him standing in the clubhouse, sweat pouring down his red face, working himself into a lather over his imagined failure to make a good impression on his top client. "We're having dinner later and I'd like to be able to tell him something specific," he said.

"Just tell Mr. Granger that everything's on schedule and he doesn't need to worry."

"Do you have that flow chart you made up that shows the closing process and everything that happens?"

"Ye-es." She glanced at Drew. He was leaning on his board, looking out at the ocean. She hoped he wasn't getting impatient.

"I'll give you a number to fax it to," Spence said. "I'll give it to Granger at dinner. He's wild for any kind of chart or graph."

"I don't have a fax machine right here."

"Then e-mail it to the office. I'll have Tabitha print it out and fax it."

Drew glanced over at her. She waved. "Uncle Spence, can't this wait?" she asked. "I'm really busy with something else right now."

"How long will it take you to e-mail that chart? And one call to the title company isn't so much to ask." He sighed, sounding sad. "I'm really counting on you, Sara. It's not like you to let me down."

Every word was like another bucketful of sand being poured over her, burying her in guilt. She swallowed hard. "Okay. I'll see what I can do."

She hung up. So much for a carefree afternoon of romance. "Is something wrong?" Drew returned to her side. "You look upset."

"I'm sorry, I have to go," she said. She replaced the phone in her bag, avoiding his eyes. "Something's come up at the office...I'm sorry."

"You can't let someone else take care of it?" he asked.

She shook her head. "No. I'd better go."

She could feel his gaze on her, intense and probing, and disappointment dragged at her. He was such a great guy. They could have had fun together…. She shook her head. "It was great meeting you," she said. Lame words, full of regret for what might have been.

"Yeah. Maybe I'll see you around."

"Yeah." Except she'd be too mortified to go anywhere near him again.

Surfboard tucked under his arm, he strode across the sand. She watched him go, suppressing a sigh. Drew was just too perfect. She'd blown it. Lost her chance. She was doomed to a life chained to her computer.

MILLS & BOON

Blaze

On sale 1st August 2008

BAD BEHAVIOUR
by Kristin Hardy

Dominick Gordon thinks his eyes are playing tricks on him when he spots Delaney Philips – it's been almost twenty years since they dated as teenagers. Still, Dom's immediate feelings show he's all grown up...and so is Delaney!

WILD CHILD
by Cindi Myers

Sara Montgomery needs this vacation in the biggest way. But getting unplugged from the mobile phone and laptop is proving tricky. Luckily for her, sexy surfer Drew Jamison arrives as the perfect distraction...

MEN AT WORK
by Karen Kendall, Cindi Myers and Colleen Collins

When these construction hotties pose for a charity calendar, more than a few pulses go through the roof! Three sexy stories in one *very* hot collection. Don't miss it!

UNDERNEATH IT ALL
by Lori Borrill

Lottery winner Nicole Reavis has the world at her feet, but all she wants is Atlanta bachelor Devon Bradshaw. The Southern charmer has plenty to teach Nicole about the finer things...including the route to his bedroom.

This proud man must learn to love again

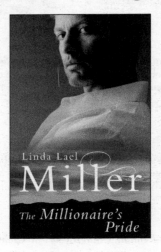

Linda Lael
Miller
The Millionaire's
Pride

Successful, rich widower Rance McKettrick is determined that nothing is going to get in the way of his new start in life.

But after meeting the sweet, beautiful Echo Wells, Rance finds her straightforward honesty is challenging everything he thought he knew about himself. Both Rance and Echo must come to grips with who they really are to find a once-in-a-lifetime happiness.

Available 18th July 2008

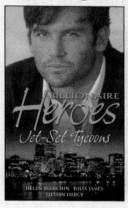

Queens of Romance

Bedding His Virgin Mistress

Ricardo Salvatore planned to take over Carly's company, so
why not have her as well? But Ricardo was stunned when in
the heat of passion he learned of Carly's innocence…

Expecting the Playboy's Heir

American billionaire and heir to an earldom, Silas Carter is
one of the world's most eligible men. Beautiful Julia Fellowes
is perfect wife material. And she's pregnant!

Blackmailing the Society Bride

When millionaire banker Marcus Canning decides it's time
to get an heir, debt-ridden Lucy becomes a convenient wife.
Their sexual chemistry is purely a bonus…

Available 5th September 2008

Collect all 10 superb books in the collection!

Celebrate 100 years
of pure reading pleasure
with Mills & Boon®

To mark our centenary, each month we're
publishing a special 100th Birthday Edition.
These celebratory editions are packed with extra
features and include a FREE bonus story.

Plus, you have the chance to enter a fabulous
monthly prize draw. See 100th Birthday Edition
books for details.

Now that's worth celebrating!

July 2008

**The Man Who Had Everything
by Christine Rimmer**
Includes FREE bonus story *Marrying Molly*

August 2008

Their Miracle Baby by Caroline Anderson
Includes FREE bonus story *Making Memories*

September 2008

Crazy About Her Spanish Boss by Rebecca Winters
Includes FREE bonus story
Rafael's Convenient Proposal

Look for Mills & Boon® 100th Birthday Editions at
your favourite bookseller or visit
www.millsandboon.co.uk

2 FREE

BOOKS AND A SURPRISE GIFT!

We would like to take this opportunity to thank you for reading this Mills Boon® book by offering you the chance to take TWO more special selected titles from the Blaze® series absolutely FREE! We're also makir this offer to introduce you to the benefits of the Mills & Boon® Read Service™—

- ★ **FREE home delivery**
- ★ **FREE gifts and competitions**
- ★ **FREE monthly Newsletter**
- ★ **Exclusive Reader Service offers**
- ★ **Books available before they're in the shops**

Accepting these FREE books and gift places you under no obligation buy, you may cancel at any time, even after receiving your free shipmer Simply complete your details below and return the entire page to th address below. You don't even need a stamp!

YES! Please send me 2 free Blaze books and a surprise gift understand that unless you hear from me, I will receive 4 supe new titles every month for just £3.15 each, postage and packing free. I a under no obligation to purchase any books and may cancel n subscription at any time. The free books and gift will be mine to keep any case.

K8ZE

Ms/Mrs/Miss/Mr ....Initials ....

BLOCK CAPITALS PLEAS

Surname ....

Address ....

....

....Postcode...........................

Send this whole page to:
UK: FREEPOST CN81, Croydon, CR9 3WZ